What You Don't Expect from Me

Also by Mat Guillan

Lo que no esperan de mi (2021)
Diario de Tayrona (2021)
Leche fría para almorzar (2021)
En busca del robot poeta (2019)

WHAT YOU DON'T EXPECT FROM ME

a novel

---

by Mat Guillan

translation by Nathaniel Kennon Perkins

Trident Press
Boulder, CO

For Laura, Oscar, and Hernán
for your example and freedom.

I'm a creep
I'm a weirdo
What the hell am I doing here?
I don't belong here

—Radiohead

The characters, places, and brands
mentioned in this book
are part
of the author's imagination.
They're not real.
The only thing that's real
is that you're touching the page,
your eyes gliding over these words,
and, more than anything, what begins to happen
inside you,
starting
now.

I don't want to be here, dealing with myself. I want to rip off my own head, hold it by the hair, and empty it out. Let my eyes go blank. Since I was a kid, people have been telling me to let things go. As though they saw me dragging a backpack full of rocks. But the real problem is who I am inside. The inner me.

"Moving out of your comfort zone can be extremely traumatic," my psychologist told me. "It's time for you to try to find yourself in the place where you are now." Then she told me that, in order to navigate this latest life change, we would use a new treatment method: "We need you to unload everything you're holding inside you. Writing can help a lot."

"But what do I write?" I asked.

"What you're feeling."

"Most of the time I don't know what I'm feeling."

"Okay. Well, write what you feel, and when you don't know what you feel, describe what's happening to you, daily occurrences, things you remember from your childhood, everything. Unload," she told me, again.

Sitting on the parquet floor of my new bedroom, I opened one of the boxes. I was sure Lourdes had packed it because it contained my old red Tamagotchi. Screen blank. Dead. The kind of gift you got a child to stop him crying. Now that I think about it, when I was seven, the Tamagotchi was my first friend. I recently heard that some Japanese kids had killed themselves because their Tamagotchis died. I'd had another sort of problem as a kid: I cried because I thought I'd never learn how to read. My classmates all knew how, but I couldn't do it. I'd take a section from the newspaper to my room and, without knowing how to put letters together or form words, I'd "read" it. I was convinced I would learn if I imitated the posture my dad sat in to read at breakfast.

While shaking my dying Tamagotchi in frustration, I'd suddenly started doing it—I don't remember how—putting syllables together, fascinated that I could suddenly read everything. I started reading street signs when we walked or drove, the flyers that arrived at the house or that people handed us on the sidewalk. Anything. I didn't stop for a second. At first, I read out loud, but then my mom told me I should read silently, in my head, and she gave me the instruction manuals for our kitchen appliances so I'd shut up. I can't blame her. I had ants in my pants. I was unbearable. I talked all the time and to everyone. I might bring up any topic at any moment. I didn't understand the concepts of discretion or a family circle of trust. I was just little. I wasn't doing it on purpose.

They gave me Ritalin, too, because I couldn't pay attention in school. The blue ceramic kitchen tiles and my mom, still sober then, illuminated by the cold morning light, pretending my spoon was an airplane delivering a hidden load of cargo to my mouth. The school bus honking outside and her chasing me through the house. She'd catch me and squeeze my cheeks, saying, "Swallow! Swallow!" That's how, in time, I quit talking, quit bothering people. Just quit.

I didn't like school. It bored me. I didn't fit in. There I was, alone and quiet, the perfect student. My language teacher was an old lady with dirty fingernails she tapped on her desk. She had lipstick on her teeth. When she was tired, she'd ask us to write about what we'd done over the weekend, and she'd always call on me to read. I invented picnic outings and soccer games with my dad, and sometimes I'd write about a yellow lab, illuminated by the sun's shining rays, trotting toward me with a tennis ball in his mouth. Or I'd say that we walked through the Parque de la Costa amusement park hand in hand, but that the excursion ended with a zombie attack. We'd all died. Even though I hadn't exactly done what she'd asked, Mrs. Genoveva would praise me.

Acting like a little weirdo kept me isolated, but one day that came to an end. Every time the teacher turned to the blackboard, something would hit me on the back of the head. It started with balls of wadded-up paper, then turned into little taps or sometimes a full open-handed slap. Once, I made the mistake of tattling to the principal, who then appeared in the classroom to give a speech about camaraderie and good manners. I ended up in the bathroom with a bloody nose, the gym teacher handing me cotton balls. I tasted blood for the first time, watching thin red threads circling down the drain of the sink. My blue sweater stained with splotches of violet. The school called my parents a thousand times.

They had the bright idea to sign me up for Taekwondo, which seemed like the perfect combination of exercise and harmonious movement. They must have thought it would help me learn to defend myself. The teacher was a kind of Jackie Chan army man who shouted orders in a heavy Chinese accent. Before class was over, he organized final battles. The parents would have shown up by then, and they watched in terror. However, it was also clear that they swelled with pride when their child landed an *ap chagi* and knocked their opponent to the ground. I didn't even want to be there, much less fight. I let myself get punched and kicked in order to bring humiliation, class by class, upon my father, whose idea it had been in the first place. The car ride home was always silent.

At school, I was slow to defend myself until one particularly bad day when I stabbed Mario, who had the habit of spitting on me. I stuck a drawing compass into his hand. With the blackboard in the background, I saw Red's face deform in surprise. I'd suddenly become a violent boy, but at least that was the end of Taekwondo, and now the other kids respected me. The blood-spattered compass changed everything. It linked me to Mario and Red forever.

Now I'm older, and that's all in the past. I cut off my head to pour out what was inside of it because, from one day to the next, we moved to the country club.

"New year, new house," my mother said, smiling, as if she were acting in a television commercial. I'd had everything in my old neighborhood, and eventually I'd stopped wondering whether people came over because there was a pool and snacks or because they were really my friends. Mostly, I'd had what I cared most about. I was near the guys and Naty.

Here, my room is my space. It's bigger than my old one, and I haven't left it since yesterday, when we got here. We don't have internet yet, or cable, or anything, and living in the real world sucks. This isolation, with no escape into TV or cyberspace, is the headquarters where I liquify my anger, staring at the ceiling. I can't sleep. Silence is anxiety. The line of light under the door and the sound of footsteps on the stairs make me uneasy. I curl into the fetal position, but it's no use. Sleep won't take me. I toss and turn, lying on one side, then the other, face down, face up, nothing. Maybe I miss the sound of the 146 bus's rumbling engine outside my window at all hours of the day and night. I don't know.

Outside, it's like the houses have been set up in the middle of a golf course. Every once in a while, I can hear the sound of a motorcycle, a lawnmower, a pool filter kicking on. Downstairs, my mother, possessed by the spirit of the Führer, shouts orders, and I know Lourdes is running back and forth, cleaning everything. The moving crew is still bringing stuff in. I still haven't opened most of my boxes.

I feel lonely, which I thought was just for old widows petting cats and sitting in armchairs, but it's started happening to me, too. Before, in my old neighborhood, I'd either invite the guys over or go out to find them, and that was that. Surely nobody has the time to come all the way out here. Not even Naty. I miss her. It's weird. Something is happening and I don't know what. Or rather, nothing is happening.

If I don't call her, she doesn't call me. I have the old lady syndrome: I need someone to contact me.

On one box was written "DON'T TOUCH. FRAGILE. CDS." I unpacked it and found The Ramones' *Mondo Bizarro*. I blasted the music, as if it might call the guys to me, but no. I just heard the contents of my head dripping onto the floor.

Naty still hasn't come over. There have been text messages and a phone call, one that I made. I told her we should take advantage of the summer weather because the pool is way bigger here. There are birds that live on the roof of the house, and I'd seen fireflies the previous night.

"Remember the argument we had about whether or not fireflies had gone extinct? Well, there are some here, and they're big. They must have left the city because of the noise or something." She asked me if the spider thing was still happening. "Not at the moment," I said. "Come over."

But I didn't go back to visit either. I stayed out here doing nothing. Kicking ass in *Counter Strike*. The day before yesterday, I unpacked the big box I'd frankensteined together with tape to move my acoustic guitar, and I started playing again. It'd been a long time since I'd played. I need to get new strings. I'm not a great guitarist, but I do alright.

I'd learned with Red, sitting by campfires on the shores of Puelo Lake on a school trip we'd taken to the south, the one where we got drunk on shitty whiskey. That's where I first heard the Ramones. Red insisted that we listen to them during the whole trip there, even though the tape was worn out and sounded terrible. Every time it ended, he'd walk up the aisle of the bus, hitting everyone along the way, and sit with the driver like he was his buddy. He'd ask where we were, if the driver was tired. Then he'd praise the driver's skills and say that he too would like to spend long hours on the road because traveling was the best way to live. He'd take advantage of being up front to pop the tape back in. On one of these little trips back and forth, he returned with the case and showed us the cover: four rough-looking guys and the name of the band. Nothing more.

"This is punk," he said.

Years later, he explained that self-titled albums were the best ones. They were the rawest. When we got back home, he made a copy for me by taping over one of my mother's Valeria Lynch tapes, and he showed me the trick where you put scotch tape over the little holes so you don't have to spend money on blank tapes. The return trip took forever and everybody was exhausted, but the beginning of the tape—"Hey! Ho! Let's Go!"—got everybody excited. Even the girls pogoed in the aisle.

When the driver got sick of it, he'd put on Nino Bravo and shout, "Listen! Listen!" He stared in the rearview mirror, and Red gave him a thumbs up.

One night by the fire, I did the best I could to keep up with Red. He started to sing, "*Yo que estoy enamorado de vos / desde hace mucho tiempo / me gusta tu cuerpo esbelto / pero más me gusta lo de adentro...*"[1] 2 Minutos[2] and the shame that petrified my left hand struggled against each other and I felt like a jackass. The song was almost over and I was thinking about how I would probably never again experience a moment as horrible as this, when I looked up and saw that the girls were still there. We finished, and they applauded. They wanted us to play another.

"One more song! One more song!"

How long could we keep at it?

Red and I had a limited repertoire, and we took lengthy breaks between songs, looking out at the lake and making thoughtful faces. One of the girls, I didn't see who, requested "Fuego de noche, nieve de dia" by Ricky Martin. I was surprised that Red knew some of it, and the rest he faked or made up, I came in late on the chord changes, trying my hardest. I learned as I went, imitating the shape of Red's

---

1. A translation of the lyrics: "I, who have been in love with you / for a long time / I like your slender body / but I don't like what's on the inside."

2. 2 Minutos is an iconic Argentine punk band, formed in 1987.

hand. It sounded terrible, and our singing was even worse, but they liked it. They laughed and sang along. We were a beautiful farce.

The cold wind carried the smell of sweet smoke from somewhere. We all started looking around, trying to figure out where it was coming from, and we smiled knowingly, even though none of us had ever actually tried it. The teachers pretended not to notice because they were sick of us, the trip, sleeping in a tent, all of it. When I looked up again, most everyone had gone to bed. The few that remained huddled under blankets, some asleep, others touching each other. Red and I were alone, silent. We hadn't recognized the right moment to stop playing and try something with a girl. Together, we lifted a huge log and threw it on the fire. We stayed up watching it burn slowly, our TV for the night, flickering until we slept.

On the coldest of these magical nights, one of the few girls who stayed up late listening to us was this beautiful girl with super pale skin. She had the face of a new-born baby or a fairy. She was the only one with short hair. That bare neck belonged to Naty. She looked straight at me, snapping her fingers in applause at the end of "La hija del fletero,"[3] and I, for the first time, felt like a girl was giving me a telepathic, ultrasonic, infinite sign of attraction.

That night, I didn't make it all the way to Nino Bravo's "Libre," which had become our closing number because it signified that Red had run out of songs he knew how to play. I'd drunk *dulce de leche*-flavored liquor to embolden myself, and, once I felt buzzed enough, I told Red that my fingers hurt. I grabbed the flask of Cusenier that I had stashed, and I sat next to Naty with my blanket. Red looked at me like I was a traitor, but I ignored him. I took a swig and offered it to Naty while holding my blanket open to her. The cold of the lake blew up from the ground, and we cuddled up together. We drank to warm ourselves and I gathered more courage. With

---

3. by Patricio Rey y sus Redonditos de Ricota

our cheeks pressed together, I put my mouth close to hers. Before I could kiss her, she murmured that she had never kissed anybody before. I hadn't either, but I didn't say so.

I played poker with Lourdes. It was quite an event to go downstairs. Mostly, I stay in my shell like a snail. I was surprised she knew how to play. She'd never mentioned it in all the years I've known her. I shuffled the cards on the table and asked where she had learned. She told me she'd grown up in Paraguay, where her dad was a gambler and a drinker.

Each time it was my turn to deal, she said, surprised, with a mix of joy and a sort of sorrow for beating me, "I can't believe how much luck I'm having!"

To keep myself occupied, I shuffled and reshuffled the cards manically while asking her what else she remembered about being little. She told me about her siblings. There were nine of them, all from the same parents. That seemed like a lot to me. I couldn't imagine having the time to make and raise so many children. She smiled when I asked her to tell me, without repeating or pausing, all their names, in order. Then her face changed.

"It's been a long time since I've seen them," she said, staring at the kitchen wall.

We heard the sound of a key in the door, and she stood to clear the table. She gathered up the beans we had used as poker chips. Each represented a 10-cent coin. Walking up the stairs to my room, I told her I'd bring down the 30 pesos I owed her. She was offended. She told me it wouldn't be necessary and asked if I wanted hot chocolate and cake now or a little later.

Interacting with another human had done me some good. Bathing myself for the first time in a few days was a relief. I needed to get out of the house. Usually, I go out and skate around whenever I need a reset. It helps tire me out so I can sleep. I hadn't left the house since we'd moved in. I put on my headphones, jogged a little, then hopped on my skateboard, pushing nowhere in particular, exploring with no real goal other than just to skate. I was listening to Pearl Jam's "Do the Evolution," which always energized me. The wind hit my face and hands. I spread my fingers wide, grabbing at nothing. Then I let the bipolar shuffle of music overcome me while an old lady with short hair, green socks, and pink leg warmers passed by, doing that kind of sporty fast walk, moving her butt in a way that seemed like it might dislocate her hips. The security guards wore Ray Bans and tried to look serious like Texas rangers. I could feel the afternoon sun slowcooking me through my black clothes. A shirtless guy with muscles and tattoos cleaned his black 4x4 truck. A little tottering boy who seemed like his son played in the front yard, a windup car in one hand and a shovel in the other. He started walking into the street. I leaned my body to the left, getting serious, Beastie Boys' "Sure Shot" playing in the background, and I crouched low and spread my arms wide to slalom around the kid. I knew there was no chance I'd hit him. I saw him as a moving obstacle and dodged him easily. I passed him and looked back. The wind blew my hair.

While polishing the tires, his father said, "Tommy, stay on the sidewalk."

It was weird to be skating and not have a dog chase after me. More than once, I'd fallen while trying to kick a dog that had been pursuing me for a half a block, but once I was on the ground, terrified of being torn to shreds, the dog calmed down and trotted away. Country club dogs didn't leave the boundaries of their yards.

In the gutter was a dying bird, chirping like it was saying its last words. A few feet away, a brindle boxer whimpered. Something was keeping it from moving forward. Every time he tried to take a step, he yelped and quivered, looking intently at the bird then up at me. Something weird was attached to its collar. He whimpered again, trying to take another step. He tried to remove the collar with his paws. Maybe he had tortured the bird all he could, but somehow the bird had escaped to a safe zone only three feet away. They were both suffering. The bird wasn't going to survive. Better to put it out of its misery. Slowly, I approached it.

It was a starry night. On my way back, I passed by the same spot. The brindle boxer was no longer wagging its tail. We could never have a dog or anything else that needed to be taken care of. Neither of my parents make any effort to care for anything or anyone. Lourdes is the only one. She always used to prepare herbal teas for me and apply compresses when I had a fever. My parents are only able to tell other people what needs to be done. No one yields to anyone else, and I don't either.

By the time I got back I was starving. Dinner was being put on the table. Noodles bolognese. We made up a triangle of terror, our own self-made torture chamber. My father poured himself more wine and said, "Paramaribo," answering the question on a TV game show. Something of my mom's fell to the ground with a metallic clatter. It was her open pill case. My father slurped his noodles. The white pills bounced over the hardwood floor until they came to rest, waiting for a mouth to swallow them. Lourdes bent down to pick them up. My mother took a long drink, her expression blank, as though bidding farewell to reality. It was the kind of silence that always preceded an explosion. We tried to draw it out as long as we could.

I felt like time was slipping away, like I was sinking into an hourglass. Just as my head was about to go under, I watched my father fill his glass to the brim. He turned up the TV, cut himself a piece of bread, used it to mop up some sauce, and continued to chew, immutable. I wound the noodles around my fork like I was winding up the timebomb that would end everything. The atomic blast that would free us from this minefield we called a family.

last night I dreamed about spiders again
lying in my new bed
hundreds of spiders
hanging from the ceiling
fell onto me

                    fell onto me

                                        fell onto me

fell onto me

                    fell onto me

                                        fell onto me

fell onto me

                    fell onto me

                                        fell onto me

fell onto me

                    fell onto me

                                        fell onto me

I went to see Mario. He said I only thought about him when my stash was getting low.

"I hope you're not getting into pills, now that you're surrounded by yuppies. They like pills over there, fancy boy."

I don't take pills. He doesn't either, but he's always getting them for somebody else. Mario always does what other people aren't willing to. I don't take pills because when I was little they were hard for me to swallow. Lourdes used to crush aspirin with a spoon and dissolve it in sugar water so I could take it. I should wear a t-shirt that says, "I'm a spoiled crybaby. Love me anyway."

It's been more than a year since I quit stealing my mom's liquid Klonopin. I'd wake up zombified. I felt suspended in time and space, stupefied. Sometimes, to relax, I smoke. My psychologist knows this but doesn't say anything. I smoke, put on an album—lately it's been Morphine's *The Night*, the last gift Naty gave me—and eventually fall asleep with my headphones on.

Doing it without anybody else noticing is easy. Between her red wine, Klonopin, and other pills, you'd have to be really lucky to find my mom sober. Plus, she has nasal polyps and can't smell anything.

With my dad, it was enough to catch him in his car with another woman. I found him parked a few blocks away from the University, and I approached. The woman, looking scared, tried to wave me away as if I were a window cleaner, or one of those guys you paid to "watch" your car. I knocked on the drivers' side window, and he looked at me coldly. When I walked away, my innocent bird brain told me not to turn around, but to wait for him to come running after me like they do in telenovelas, but no.

Later that night, I was smoking a post-dinner digestif, sure my parents were asleep, when he opened my bedroom door without knocking. We were still living in the other house then, and I wasn't exactly crying over the disintegrating family ties. I was searching for amateur porn on the internet. My browser window flickered. After that, I started locking my bedroom door.

My father had either come to explain the situation or to lie to me—it didn't really matter which—but when he saw me he screwed up his face and kept quiet. He knew well that him opening his big mouth was nothing compared to me opening mine. I smoked like a recently fired gun, and—like father, like son—we did what we were best at: neither of us said anything. That moment's hypocritical glances were enough to form a pact. I wouldn't tell my mother, and neither would he. He wouldn't do his thing in front of her, and neither would I. Easy. He slowly closed the door, and my *Nevermind* poster swung back into view. The baby trying to grab the underwater dollar calmed me.

One morning, a few days later, my mother pounded on my door. Her shouting woke me. Lost in the morning's mental fog, I was sure the traitor had ratted me out. When I opened the door, she told me I had to see what had happened to the front door. She was acting all mysterious. Still sleepy, I asked what it was while I pulled on a pair of pants.

My dad had bought me a brand new car, a bribe I accepted gladly. A car could be useful if I ever wanted to escape.

It was the first time I left the country club. I'm not sure exactly how long the drive back to my old neighborhood took, but it wasn't quick. I did some mental math and realized I had listened to *One Hot Minute* by Red Hot Chili Peppers all the way through and then started it over. I remember having crazily drummed along to "Coffee Shop" on the steering wheel, so it had been about an album and a half. It took more than an hour to get to Mario's house. We bumped fists. Red was there too. Mario had told him I was coming.

"What's up, Richie Rich? All good? How's the Country Club, dude? Can I play in your yard?"

Mario is older than we are. He was held back in high school. He got in trouble, lost his virginity, and smoked in the bathroom. He did everything before we did. He was living at his grandma's house. Now, he lives there alone because his grandma died. Nobody knew anything about his parents, and a mix of respect and fear kept us from asking. I remember one summer night when he took us out to an abandoned railroad. Without a word, he took out a pistol and started shooting at a rusted boxcar. A few of the other guys wanted to shoot, and he taught them how. I didn't want to, but I felt a rush of adrenaline. Mario shot without blinking. He clenched his teeth and didn't move a muscle.

I asked where he had gotten the piece, and he said, "Santa Claus brought it. You want to shoot?"

From the beginning it was clear Mario was the leader of our group. Somehow we always ended up doing whatever he had already done. He dropped out of high school after his one true love Andrea Di Marco slapped him at the end-of-year dance, but that's not the reason behind the one and only time we stopped hanging out with him. Red had stood up to Mario for thinking he was the boss of us. We were no longer only going to do what he told us to, always under the threat of being called a bunch of pussies. Red wasn't wrong, of course, but the situation bothered him more than it did anyone else. He felt overshadowed. The two of them spat on and insulted one another, and we had to pull them apart so they wouldn't try to knock each other out.

Red was always the one to approach a group of girls first, and we would follow, but Mario had this sort of mercenary, no-limits mindset that fascinated us. A few of the guys were on Red's side because we needed someone to follow when Mario wasn't around. Plus, he lived in my neighborhood. His house was on the corner, and our mothers got along well. I was allowed to sleep over.

Two months went by in which Mario didn't wait for us after school, sitting astride that beat-to-shit Aurora folding bike he had. We rode around on our BMX bikes, and sometimes a girl would stand on Red's pegs. Every now and then, one of the rest of us would have a girl to bring along, and the sun would shine, and we would hate being virgins.

One afternoon we showed up to that same abandoned railroad with Red. He was going to fight an older boy who'd made out with his girlfriend. Before long, Red was getting the shit beat out of him and none of the rest of us wanted to jump in because we thought we'd end up the same way. Two shots rang out, and Mario appeared like a cowboy.

"Want to taste lead?" he asked the older guys, who were terrified. One of them took off running. It was funny later, but at the time it was scary. I felt like he was capable of killing us all.

"Listen up. Nobody lays a finger on my friend. You get close and I shoot. Simple. Get some," he said, in the way that he alone could talk to the world. We froze for a couple seconds, and then things got worse. "Let's go, shitheads," he shouted, and shot over the older guys' heads, at the train. There was the sound of metal hitting metal, and they ran while Mario smiled, like it was all a game.

From that day on, we never split up again. I'd been missing that grimy mattress on the floor that he had instead of a couch. *Loco Live* was playing in the background. I tried to get the conversation going.

"What's been going on with you, Red?"

Sometimes we seem like a self-help group.

He said he'd exchanged blows with his father while trying to defend his mom, and that he hadn't been showing up for his shifts at the record store.

Mario had a question for me: "Look, I'm sorry to have to ask, but I'll cut to the chase. I gotta bring it up because you always play everything so close to the chest, but how is it that your old man got so much money from one day to the next? Did he win the lottery?"

A song had just ended, and the silence felt extreme. It only lasted a few seconds, but the mysterious awkwardness of the moment bothered me.

"He's a politician, or a proxy for them, a *testaferro*, a straw man, that kind of shit," I said.

They stayed quiet, maybe out of pity, until Joey broke the silence with another "One, Two, Three, Four!" Mario turned it up, and we nodded along to the most moving music known to man.

some
times
when, late, late at night,
I can't sleep
I feel like I owe this world
some
thing

Finally, Naty came out to the country club. There was astonishment in her eyes as I showed her around the luxurious house, and I felt ashamed in a way I hadn't before. Being well off is one thing, but having a little TV in the bathroom so you can see who's at the door while you're sitting on the toilet is another. My mother appeared and, without even saying hello, started scolding her for not coming around more often. She asked why she hadn't come over before now, said that she looked skinnier and that she liked her hair more than how she'd had it before. She concluded by telling Naty that the only time the family was truly complete was when she was there. When I was a kid, she used to ask me to call all of her friends "auntie," friends who have since vanished off the face of the earth. She was treating Naty like my girlfriend.

Everybody thinks she's my girlfriend, actually. We're always together and we do all the things that boyfriends and girlfriends do, but neither of us has ever tried to define anything. We don't celebrate anniversaries or anything like that. We started going out a little, seeing movies, listening to music together, and one day her dad died and we cried together. At the funeral she didn't talk to anyone else but me. Not even her mom. To me, that seemed important. We love each other a lot, that much is clear. But we don't say those three words.

In the afternoon, we went out to the pool. My mother insisted on coming along with a glass in her hand. She took her medicine, her teeth turned red, and she transformed. Naty, sunbathed in a lounge chair in her bikini, hiding behind her sunglasses while my mother talked. A helicopter flew over the country club. All three of us looked to the sky. I jumped in the pool. I stayed underwater until I couldn't hear my mom anymore, kicking hard. I wanted to drown, or to be devoured by the giant shark that had tormented my childhood dreams, dyeing the water red like it was an enormous pool of wine, into which my mom would perform a swan dive.

After midnight, after sex and the ecstatic comedown, I was in that strange cotton world between consciousness and sleep when I felt something tickle my scapula. Massacre[1] was playing low.

Naty leaned over me and whispered "I'm reading you backwards."

What had started as a soft caress while I was sleeping had turned into Naty popping a zit. It's gross, but she loves it. She sees one, and as soon as she has the chance, she squeezes and tells me to relax.

"If you squirm, that just makes it worse. Sshhh, there it goes, it's done, it's done. See? Look." She smiled and showed me. I wish I could drain myself of all the pus that was inside of me that way.

I woke up later to find her standing in front of the window, nude, the light of the moon silhouetting her rail-thin body and coming through the peephole between her skinny legs. Silently, I moved to stand behind her in my boxers. I've spent the last few nights looking out at the country club. There's something about it. I don't know exactly what. I spend a while trying to see if there's some insomniac out for a walk, or if something is going on. Anything. I hugged her from behind, resting my chin on her shoulder.

We stood quietly, looking out into the darkness. Suddenly, I saw moving lights by the golf course.

"Look," I said, and pointed.

By the way they moved, it was clear they were flashlights, bouncing quickly, like part of a nighttime game where people run around shouting ridiculously.

---

1. the Argentine skate-punk band

"Let's go check it out," she said.

"Check what out?"

"I don't know. Whatever's going on.

"Think we should?"

"Yeah, let's go," she said, pulling on her t-shirt and flower-printed skirt. No underwear.

She grabbed her purse and said, "Let's go. Come on. Let's go, let's go."

Walking down the stairs, she took my hand firmly. Stealthily, we opened and closed the door. The smell of grass and wet dirt woke me all the way up. There wasn't anybody in the street. We walked three blocks, exchanging occasional glances and laughing. Flashes of blue light bounced off the trees. A security guard's car turned the corner. We hid. We didn't want to have to explain anything. We stumbled and fell into a ditch, which was mostly dry, luckily, filled with a cushion of soft grass. She kissed me. Tongue. It was the best. I raised her gauzy skirt and touched her slowly, despite my excitement. Her lips. My wet fingers moving slowly prompted a short, sharp moan. The adrenaline in the contraction of my testicles, in her warm hand moving over my pubic hair. I'd never had sex outdoors, and doing so there, in the grass, maybe with some security camera focusing on us, entwined like an apparition of bizarre creatures, lit us on fire. But we heard a dog growling, not six feet away, on the other side of a hedge. I very much wanted to keep going—"It doesn't matter, it doesn't matter"—but they didn't have that particular dog in mind when they coined the phrase "man's best friend." He started to howl like a wolf, and we returned to our search for the lights.

As we got further away from the houses and closer to the golf course, the country club grew more desolate. A breeze rippled the hem of her skirt, and the moon made her legs even whiter. I wanted to kneel down and use them as a scarf. I stopped walking, and when she turned to see what I was doing, I kissed her hard on the mouth, the face, an eye, her ear, I bit her neck. I tried to touch her again, but doing it while standing in the middle of the street wasn't quite the same. She held my hands and gave me little kisses, trying to calm me. I didn't know how to turn back time to when we were in the ditch, wet, the dog growling. Take out a steak and throw it as far as possible, the dog bounding off, surprised by his good fortune. And we'd get lucky too. But there was nothing I could do except quit kissing her and steal Cobain's most famous line.

"With the lights off, it's less dangerous," I murmured shyly.

I spotted some bushes by the man-made lake that looked like they might make a suitable shelter for us. She smiled and stepped back to look through her purse. I hadn't thought to bring condoms. I was surprised by what I saw when she pulled her hand out. Not only were there condoms, plus the normal lipstick and whatever, but Naty had a can of spray paint in there.

I woke up because "Anxiety" was playing. Someone was calling me. This is part of my self-care: my phone plays a song telling me anxiety makes me happy. I didn't know where my phone was. I looked around and I found it under my bed, inside a shoe. I answered quickly, desperately, thinking it might be Naty. The previous night had ended with a fight.

When she'd finished spray painting the asphalt, I was no longer smiling. I realized that, just like the security cameras might have spied us having sex, they'd also be able to spot the tagging. I was scared. I started walking backwards, like I'd seen a monster, and I told her we should get out of there. She followed me.

Walking quickly in the still night, I asked her, "Why do you even have that?"

From there, everything turned sour. I was horrible, saying things I didn't mean, reinforcing every possible reason that she might have had to not want to see me again. All because I never learned how to communicate. People like me shouldn't be allowed to have a tongue. It should be cut out at birth, along with the umbilical cord, and thrown to the pigs. Silence is the safest place.

This whole time we'd gone without seeing each other was because Naty had gotten involved in political activism. She told me it'd been the past two months, but it must have been at least four because she'd been acting weird for a while. She messaged me, saying, "I didn't want to tell you." She knew I'd react badly to the political stuff, so she left in the early hours of the morning.

You can't trust a single politician, Natalia. They're all

liars. I live with one! I know what I'm talking about! No, Natalia. I don't know how to believe in a better world. Can't you see it's more rotten every day? Can't you see that we're also rotten? I don't know how to believe in anything or anybody. I eat as much tuna as I can. Fuck the dolphins. But go right ahead. Get radicalized. That's what everybody in that fucking university does. Get high for the first time with some other guy. Do it.

The phone call, which smelled like my own stale feet, was from my mother.

"I'm calling because I've been at the house all morning, knocking on your door, but you won't answer," she complained. She was sober, but she seemed wound up. She said, "What's your email address? I don't have one, and my yoga teacher needs to send me some information about the class."

In the background, I could hear someone else's voice. It wasn't Lourdes. I wanted to tell her to open her own account, but I started to imagine all the work and torment that would mean for me, and something in my rotten heart prompted me to give her my address. The email came a little later. I printed it out and taped it to her bedroom door, thereby relieving myself of any further responsibility.

Walking to her bedroom, I heard indignant shouting. She said something about how she couldn't believe it, it just couldn't be, we'd moved to this neighborhood because it was safe, and now this had happened. I couldn't understand much. Someone else was talking, but I couldn't hear what they were saying. I picked up the telephone but only heard the dial tone.

She said, "We should have moved to Uruguay!" and then something about how surely there would be a neighborhood meeting this week. "We'll see what the president of the board of directors has to say about the theft, but something needs to be done. Thank you, thank you," and she closed the door.

Curiosity drew me to the window. I couldn't make out what was being said. I opened the curtains a little to spy. A group of neighbors was walking away from the front door, heading in the direction of the clubhouse, gesticulating.

Still a little dazed, half asleep, I sat in front of the computer. "Yogabriela" greeted me in the chat. I didn't answer. Her profile picture was just a yin-yang. The last thing I needed was for my mother to want to use my computer to chat with her new teacher. Jesus Christ, what a pain. I closed the window and looked through the news and found it. News travels fast. Yuppie town, giant hell.

Headline: "Another Country Club Robbery." A house had been broken into. For the victim's safety, it didn't say whose. Nobody had been home, and only money had been taken. The most interesting part of the article was what the thieves had supposedly done in the house. They ate, drank, left all the faucets running (just like in *Home Alone*, I thought), and threw the sofas, television, and various other pieces of furniture into the pool. I turned on the TV. The coverage on the channel owned by one of the media moguls who lives in the country club pointed out that graffiti had also been found on one of the neighborhood streets. This was also attributed to the thieves. The reporter noted that the security cameras hadn't been functioning. He reiterated several times that the spray paint was red. A symphonic soundtrack underscored an atmosphere of tragedy. Then, in a grave voice, the reporter cast doubt on the security of gated communities and promised to follow up with further details.

We
no
longer
repress
the
sexual

.

We
repress
the
sentimental

.

"You're aware that you're making very intimate information public, right?" my psychologist asked me, writing on her notepad.

She'd read what I'd written and was surprised to see that I've been publishing my therapy treatment online, making my life story available, even if under a pseudonym. She worried things might slip out of my hands. Every time I sit on her leather sofa and feel the intense warmth of her previous patient, I get ready to expose my private self to her, and when I open my mouth I do so without the anonymity of the internet. I'm not sure what's worse, doc.

"You did very well to get out a little," she said, changing the topic. "Lack of sunlight can have a negative impact on mood. We can't fall back into that habit. Your life has to continue to develop."

She didn't care what had happened with Naty, but it's keeping me awake at night. I obsess about returning to that moment, about not having said the things I did. I want to erase it from our memories, like an extremely hungover morning in which you can't remember how you got home the night before. I don't have any strategies for anything. I play Risk quietly, but aggressively. One die against five, excited, kamikaze. I do what I can how I can.

I'm not going to try to be an angry tough guy, waiting for her to reach out, a message or call, a signal of any kind. When my mom called and my phone was ringing and I was desperately searching for it, I had thrown away all strategy. It's time to stick my pride up my ass. I need to see her. I don't care if she's become radicalized. She could be an activist for the Ku Klux Klan for all I cared. She could throw newborn babies into a pit full of hungry dragons. I need to be with her, to make love, to blow up condoms like balloons and try to keep them from touching the ground. Something to make me curl up and fall asleep, as defeated as if I have come home from war.

The alarm clock's red lines said 03:30. Every time I looked at the time, it was a palindrome. It was unbearably hot, but that wasn't all. I didn't know what to do. Something was making me anxious, but I wasn't sure what. Outside was hell. I should have a hamster wheel, but I don't, so I tore apart my bedroom, undoing all the straightening up Lourdes had done. Little by little, my room returned to its normal state. I found a little crumb of a nug, as precious as gold, and my inner hamster jumped up and down. I sat at the computer and moved the mouse. The monitor turned on and illuminated my face with the divine light of the virtual world. Don't blame me. I'm part of the generation that doesn't use the telephone as a telephone. We praise God for having invented text messages and chat. Naty wasn't connected. Neither were the guys.

Then, an irresistible "Hello." My mom's yoga teacher greeted me. I hadn't even put any music on yet. I thought she might tell me something having to do with my mom, but she asked me if I exercised, if I went to the gym. She told me it was important to take care of your body because it was the only one you got. The night didn't promise much lucidity. I didn't even finish responding, and she was writing another message, then another, and another.

I felt like she was about to try to get me to sign up for classes, and I wrote, "I can't stand health evangelists."

Yogabriela wrote, "I'm going to be your nightmare, kid."

I needed to change the subject, so I asked her what music she was listening to at that moment. Portishead. I imagined a woman my mother's age slumped on the living room couch, listening to Portishead, spilling wine on her bathrobe, and burping in solitude. Portishead. Weird. I expected her to recommend something Indian, sitars and trancelike hand drums.

Yogabriela: Do you like Portishead, or what?

Playmobile: It's fine, but it's late and I'm a boy who's lost in a forest darker than night.

Yogabriela: Admit that you were the burglar. Turn yourself in!

Playmobil: Uh-oh. You caught me. You have to watch out for strangers.

Yogabriela: You don't scare me even a little, kid.

Playmobil: It's too hot to scare anyone. It's the worst.

Yogabriela: It's horrible. I can't sleep, so I went on a voyage.

Playmobil: Huh?

Yogabriela: I've been drinking caipirinhas since dinner, and now I'm in Brazil dancing the samba. So do me the favor of forgetting everything we're talking about.

Playmobil: Caipirinhas and Portishead? Tristeza nao tem fim. I have the air conditioning turned all the way up, but it's still unbearable. I could use a caipirinha. I'd pour it on my head and use the refrigerator like a coffin. I want it to be wintertime.

Yogabriela: Shut up. When it's winter you probably want it to be summer.

Playmobil: No way. I hate people who want it to be summer, like we live in Rio de Janeiro or something. We live in Buenos Aires. Humidity and sweat. Long live the cold!

Yogabriela: You want it to be cold so you have to do something to warm up, right? Hahahaha. Sorry.

Playmobil: Adult language and nudity.

Yogabriela: Is it time to send the kid to bed?

And we went on like that. Eventually I told her that if she had anything she wanted me to pass on to my mom, I'd be happy to do so.

I'm Alf.

I'm an adorable doormat.

She was telling me about her activism. They met at a spot near the Palace of Congress. "We're going to finish up some banners," she'd written when I reached out about getting together. I bottled up my jealousy. I clenched my teeth. Before logging off, she'd said, "Come if you want, and we'll go out afterwards," and she gave me the address. I thought, if I go, it's because I'm keeping tabs on her; if I don't go, it's because I don't care. Either way, she invited me. I didn't know what to do until my jealousy broke through my clenched teeth, pushing me out the door. Okay, I'll go. It's not such a bad idea. I'll pick her up at her activist hangout. Great. Real mature. In a way, I was showing her, despite my many limitations, that I was accepting this new, revolutionary version of her.

Listening to *Modern Life is Rubbish* by Blur while driving into the capital, I had a kind of revelation: Blur was the soda pop evolution of the Clash. I know nobody cares about that, but that's what took my mind back to the "Coffee and TV" video and the little animated milk carton. All those songs about hating modern life. All those hours shut in watching television, *Dragon Ball, SilverHawks, The Simpsons*, infomercials, late nights trying to hack into the Venus porn channel.

I started thinking that I should spend my whole life on that highway. Then maybe I'd figure out why Naty spent so much time in the political world, being an activist for a party. We went years without ever knowing what my dad did for work. Until, as a child, I overheard a phone call and started to understand the fancy cars, expensive clothes, and paradise vacations. However, the contrast with the rest of the world wasn't so evident in a private Catholic school. We didn't know what a student union was. We had catechism, studied the bible, took communion and confirmation because it's what everybody did. We went to mass and English class and took swimming lessons so we could learn how not to drown when we weren't with Mommy. And God was by our side. Oh, yes. The traffic in the capital brought me back to the present, and the rest of the trip turned me into the worst human on earth, annoying, miserable, and abandoned by God, honking my horn, cursing, and looking for a place to park.

I rang the doorbell. An old house, heavy iron door, cat piss smell. Nobody answered. I saw that the door was usually closed with a lock and a chain when nobody was there. There wasn't a lock. It was open. I went in. Gray walls and humidity. From the back drifted music I couldn't make out. Long hallway. A skinny guy came walking toward me. Baseball cap, beard, and backpack. I asked if Naty was there, but he didn't recognize the name.

Maybe it was because I was nervous, but I said, "A girl with short hair and a white face."

A white face?

I was holding my hand up to show how tall she was. I might as well have said, "She's of the Aryan race."

"She's upstairs," he said.

As I climbed the stairs, I realized that they were listening to "Luzbelito" by Los Redondos. I saw Naty sewing something, kneeling on the black-and-white checkerboard floor. I stood quietly for a few seconds until they noticed me. Out of 15 people, there were maybe two women. They looked at me.

"Come in, come in. Have you been standing there long?"

I introduced myself to the group and one of them shook my hand and called me "Comrade." I didn't know what to say, so I gave him a thumbs up.

It wasn't long before I needed to escape the conversation, so I went to put the kettle on and make *mate* for the first time in my life. I worried that I might have to admit where I lived, what I studied, and what I did. They didn't ask, but once the *mate* started going around, I was afraid that at any moment a question might lead in that direction. The other girl made a minimal attempt at dialogue, but I saw the look on her face, and I interrupted her, asking if the water was hot enough, if she wanted sugar.

My fear went away.

Time froze as I heard a masculine voice say, "Will you pass me some *mate*, Natu?"

I spun around. I could see every cell, every atom, dripping with libido. He wanted to fuck Naty and had no intention of hiding it. He was asking her for the *mate* that I was pouring. To him, I didn't exist. I was just a stupid extension of her. He was showing me that of course he knew who Naty was. Natu! He knew her. They were close. All this while I sat on a little stool with my "I don't know how to fit in here" expression and the thermos in my hand, like a peasant waiting for the rain. I wished the house would burst into flames, killing everyone else except Naty, who I would save heroically.

He's older. He must be almost thirty. He told her the water was a little cold, that it needed to be heated up. Clearly, when I wasn't around, he gave his comrade hugs and checked out her ass. And Naty smiling uncomfortably, pretending she was happy I'd come, trying to keep up the innocent charade that activism only did good. That she and all her comrades were there, surrounded by so much cat-piss smell, to heal the world, make it a better place for you and for me, as Michael Jackson says, instead of just hooking up late at night in a dirty bathroom.

In the car, she expressed her surprise at how few girls had shown up.

"I don't know why," she said.

I tried to be understanding, but I felt like an idiot. Or it was maybe the other way around.

"The guys seem pretty cool," I lied.

I went through my mom's bedside table drawer and found a little notepad. She makes lists. Two columns, neat, written in black ballpoint pen in uppercase print.

<table>
<tr><td>One column TO DO</td><td>and another TO BUY</td></tr>
<tr><td>Little to do.</td><td>Lots to buy.</td></tr>
</table>

"You were wasting your time anyway."

This was my mom's brilliant conclusion when I told them I wasn't interested in marketing and wanted to drop out of school. It's been a while since I stopped showing up for my classes, a fact I hadn't exactly mentioned. It's one thing to quit something and another altogether to break the news to Lady Cabernet Sauvignon and have her talk to you about wasting your time. I didn't answer.

"Honestly, I don't know why you even signed up," she said. I went up to my room while she yelled. "Where are you going? Can't you see we're talking here?" When I got to the top of the stairs I heard her say, "That boy is hopeless."

Years ago, all I cared about was that MTV existed. And BOOM, the "Smells Like Teen Spirit" video appeared. I remember the first time I saw it. Super excited, I called Red. Not only did he say he'd also seen it, but he told me that the title of the song was based on how a girl had written on a wall of Kurt Cobain's house that he smelled like women's deodorant. Then he told me that I had to see Tool's videos, a band I didn't know yet. And that's how my life was. While I was laughing my ass off at *Beavis and Butt-Head*, people started asking me what I wanted to be when I grew up, but not in the same way they had when I was a little kid. The question was, "What are you going to study?" I didn't know. I acted all punk and said that I wasn't interested in anything. Or that I wanted to be a firefighter. But the question grew more and more abominable. I still remember the faces of those Disney-brainwashed adults slyly saying the same thing my mother had: "This boy is hopeless."

In fourth grade, people from some company invaded our class without warning. Even the teachers didn't seem to know it was happening. They gave us a vocational test that consisted of multiple-choice questions. We cheered for this new way to take exams because it was easier. We didn't have to write as much. The teachers tried to convince us it was actually more difficult, as if we were idiots. They never gave us the results, but they handed an *alfajor* to everyone who finished.

I don't know where my passion is. Nothing excites me. Everything is boring. I should have gone to trade school. Attention, youth of the world! Want to learn useful stuff? Go to trade school! Don't even consider studying marketing. Marketing's greatest achievement has been to convince us we have to spend several years studying it in order to work in the field. The only thing that really captivates me is the internet, but I'm not a nerd. I chat with strangers for hours, and it's addicting. The internet enables that sort of cannibalistic voyeurism that's so enthralling. There are people from the furthest reaches of the globe who comment below what I write and publish on the internet. They ask me questions. They give me advice. Young people support me, and other parents defend my parents. We should assemble into armies like orcs and find a public square where we can fight in the mud until it dries. The other day, Venus64 commented: "You're shameless. I hope you never have kids!" I didn't know what to tell her. I responded, "Venus, thanks for the love, and most of all for the porno."

> **Yogabriela:** If I don't say hi and start a conversation, you do nothing.
> **Plamobil:** I'm a bug that lives under a rock and I only come out when someone lifts that rock.
> **Yogabriela:** Ah, okaaaay. I was just about to say that you don't seem tooo young.
> **Playmobil:** And you don't seem sooooo old.

Yogabriela: Oh, that's nice. The kid figured out sarcasm.

Playmobil: Hahahaha

Yogabriela: It's like when babies discover they have a tongue.

Playmobil: So before I was a kid, and now I'm a baby. I'm traveling backwards in time. Pretty soon you'll tell me I'm a fetus.

Yogabriela: Don't be dumb. There are two possibilities. Either you're getting older or I'm getting younger.

Playmobil: Both, I think.

Yogabriela: Hahahahaha

Playmobil: Either you're fun or I don't get out enough.

Yogabriela: Both.

Playmobil: Seriously though, you seem younger than your age.

Yogabriela: Why?

Playmobil: I don't know. You're funny. In general, older people annoy me. Mostly, they don't listen to Portishead while sharpening knives.

Yogabriela: The problem is that we always chat late and you're half asleep. What do you listen to? What are you listening to right now? And no fair lying to try to seem cool.

Playmobil: It's on shuffle. It's beautiful to live on random and know that anything at all might come along.

Yogabriela: What are you listening to? I don't want excuses. I want to see the skeletons in your closet.

Playmobil: Elvis came on shuffle, so I turned into an old man. I'm 1,000 years old and complain about everything.

Yogabriela: Blasphemy! Elvis is timeless. He's our eternal lover. There isn't a woman in the world who doesn't have a thing for Elvis.

Playmobil: Alright. Take it easy.

Yogabriela: Elvis liiiiives!

Playmobil: I've ended up blaspheming the Lord because my mom asked to borrow my email so you could send information about your yoga classes, and now here you are tying an Elvis armband around my arm.

Yogabriela: I told you I was going to be your nightmare.

Playmobil: You're the last person I talk to before I go asleep, so…

Yogabriela: Look, I sneak into dreams and nobody can stop me.

Playmobil: Hahaha. It's like those softcore porn movies where you have a futuristic headset. In this case it's an Elvis-themed one. You push a button and dream about the person in the headset, and we know where it goes from there.

Yogabriela: You're trying to get my hopes up.

Playmobil: WHAT?

Yogabriela: Every time I open my mouth shows how old I am. Don't bother. It's already late. I started without you.

Playmobil: I'm just a kid. I'm going to tell my mom.

Yogabriela: Give it a while. She'll hear your screams.

At dinner, just about the only moment we're ever all together, they told me that if I wasn't going to study, then I had to work. Really, it was my mom who said it. My dad nodded his head like one of those Chinese bobblehead dogs on car dashboards. I didn't answer. I lowered my gaze. In my mind, I celebrated naively, as if working was awesome. When I woke the next morning, I found that an envelope and the classified pages had been slid under my door. Allowing me to lock my door so they won't catch me smoking makes it seem like they trust me. But the truth is that nobody cares if I kill myself or light everything on fire while listening to Black Sabbath. They think I'm harmless, and it pisses me off. On the envelope my mom had written, "BUY YOURSELF A SUIT." In the newspaper, my mom had used a red pen to circle the jobs that she thought I would be qualified for. I didn't read them. She, whose major career success has been selling a few Avon lotions to her friends, was now my boss. She was telling me how to dress and where to work.

My only previous job had been in a call center in Martínez as a customer service representative for a cell phone company. I'd looked for a job that required the fewest possible hours so I could save money, without having to ask my parents for it, so I could go on vacation with the guys. Every time they give me money, they want to govern my life. They'd forbidden me to work, but I did it anyway. I showed up to the interview wearing a white shirt, jeans, and the lug-soled boat shoes I wore to school. That was as much as I was willing to get dressed up in order to scam a company into paying me for a little while. I didn't have any experience. I had just graduated high school.

The call center was a kind of experimental laboratory for alienated guys and girls like me, stuffed into cubicles, sitting in chairs, talking on the phone. We served as a human cushion between the company and the clientele. It was simple. The customers hated the company, and, because of that, they hated us too. In fact, by the end of my first week, I had already insulted one of them. Bonus points because he was a lawyer. After a long conversation in which he humiliated me with every strategy he had learned in college, he asked for my name and threatened to report me. I exploded.

I told him, "You're a lawyer? So, then everything you're saying is definitely a lie!"

I finished shouting and felt the silence in the call center sawing into the back of my neck.

When my shift ended, my supervisor, one of those guys that smiled like the Virgin Mary while simultaneously telling you you were the most worthless person in the world, called me in to talk.

"We listened to the call. The customer was very impolite, it's true, but you have to control the situation. First of all, you can't take anything personally. The customers aren't mad at you. They're mad at the company. In cases like these, you need to end the conversation by saying that you can't continue to be of assistance while being spoken to in such a way and that you hope he has a good day anyway."

I wanted to insult *him*. Don't take it badly. I'm not insulting you. I'm insulting company policy. Tell me to have a good day. Do it. I held back because I needed the money. They didn't fire me.

The rest of the month I was an automaton, saying good morning and good afternoon, lubricating the machine of mistreatment with my spit. But they gave us prizes. Oh, yes. There were two prizes we could win: 1) the prize for a quick response, in which the customer received a rapid and effective solution, and 2) the prize for quality of response, in which the customer was left feeling confident about using their cell phone. In other words, you couldn't ever win both prizes because with better quality came slower service, so welcome to the jungle, stinky babies.

I remember now. I'd erased it from my head. The worst part was that every two minutes I had to tell a client my made-up name, which wasn't anything more than my unfortunate middle name. Nowhere where they make you change your name can be a good place.

I was leaving yesterday when I heard my mom, already drunk, yelling at Lourdes.

"This house is filthy, *señora*! How many times do I have to tell you, *señora*?!"

But when I came downstairs and she saw me with the newspaper in hand she rejoiced. She must have thought I was going to fulfill all her desires of having an obedient son.

Earlier, when I'd first woken up, I went to the kitchen and saw that the ad I had taken out in the newspaper had been published. I'd paid for it with the suit money that had been in the envelope. I circled it in red and left it on the kitchen table:

"Young failure seeking job as chambermaid for rich old lady who is not his mother."

I feel guilty
for
some of the things
I do
and
it distresses me
.

But
what are worse
are the things
I end up doing
because
of this
guilt
.

"What's up with you?"

"Nothing."

"Tell me."

"Nothing's the matter."

Our roles were reversed. She was withdrawn, and I was asking the questions. Naty was sitting on my bed, painting her fingernails black, telling me in a monotone voice that nothing was wrong. She focused on the details of her fingernails, like I wasn't there. Without looking up, she told me to stop sniffing her fingernail polish remover, but not as a joke.

"Can you put that back where it was?" she said, scolding.

Sitting in front of my computer, I watched her stand up quickly, her back to me, looking out the window at the kids who rode their bikes around the country club all day. She waved her hands to dry her nails. I observed her, backlit, the skinny silhouette of her body, a crystal swan, beautifully fragile.

After a few days without seeing each other, our sexual encounters usually escalated from minimal contact to desperate passion, but this time was different. Like how she told me nothing was wrong, but I was sure something was. I tried to reinsert myself in her consciousness by putting my arms around her waist from behind. She pulled away, but it wasn't a game this time.

Sometimes she liked to pretend our contact was a kind of encounter between strangers. I pressured her, and she gave in gradually, looking at me shyly, complicitly, resisting less and less and letting herself be kissed with a microscopic gesture of her lips, yielding the skin of her neck to me an inch at a time while shivering with delight. I was committed to the role, waiting for the moment Naty would give herself over and bite my lips, excited and passionate, but I didn't get anything other than a hollow, sad kiss.

Resigned, almost motionless, she let me start slowly taking her clothes off, but her coldness chastened me. Feeling miniscule, I stopped, taking my hands away in slow motion, as if we had fallen asleep. After seconds that felt like centuries, she gave me an uncomfortable hug. Looking at the ceiling, I felt a strange caress that I won't be able to stop thinking about. Her fingers moving like a tarantula on my right shoulder, her fingers brushing over me with a mix of sorrow and solace.

When I was sure she had fallen asleep—when she fell asleep she always kicked her legs or twitched reflexively—I started writing on my computer. She is lying in my bed. She is letting her hair grow out. It's like she's becoming a woman in this exact moment, while I try to decipher her "nothing," try to understand what's the matter with her, feeling an abyss of insecurity open inside my head because nothing is everything.

NO, therefore I am. NO, therefore I am. NO, therefore I am.
NO, therefore I am. NO, therefore I am. NO, therefore I am.
NO, therefore I am. NO, therefore I am. NO, therefore I am.
NO, therefore I am. NO, therefore I am. NO, therefore I am.
NO, therefore I am. NO, therefore I am. NO, therefore I am.
NO, therefore I am. NO, therefore I am. NO, therefore I am.
NO, therefore I am. NO, therefore I am. NO, therefore I am.
NO, therefore I am. NO, therefore I am. NO, therefore I am.
NO, therefore I am. NO, therefore I am. NO, therefore I am.
NO, therefore I am. NO, therefore I am. NO, therefore I am.
NO, therefore I am. NO, therefore I am. NO, therefore I am.
NO, therefore I am. NO, therefore I am. NO, therefore I am.
NO, therefore I am. NO, therefore I am. NO, therefore I am.
NO, therefore I am. NO, therefore I am. NO, therefore I am.
NO, therefore I am. NO, therefore I am. NO, therefore I am.
NO, therefore I am. NO, therefore I am. NO, therefore I am.
NO, therefore I am. NO, therefore I am. NO, therefore I am.
NO, therefore I am. NO, therefore I am. NO, therefore I am.
NO, therefore I am. NO, therefore I am. NO, therefore I am.

I saw Yogabriela.

I was in the country club entrance, leaning out of my car, arguing with the security guards. They saw me every single day. How could they possibly need my information each time I went out or came in is what I wanted to know.

"You didn't check the papers of the burglars who came in last month," I said.

One of them responded in monotone, "It's the rule, sir."

I'm an android, sir.

It's my work, sir.

I'm incapable of thinking for myself, sir.

I turned up the stereo to drown him out. In the roundabout at the entrance, planted with colorful flowers, with a fountain where naked cupid statues spouted water from their mouths, a woman jogged by. Her tits bounced fabulously. She looked over and waved, smiling.

During all the time we'd spent chatting, I'd avoided the idea of sharing photos due to my own insecurities. I'd been afraid of the exchange. But I've also started to feel trapped, not knowing exactly what was on the other side of the screen. The mystery had been growing in my mind. I spent nights thinking about this exact casual encounter, wondering if it might have already happened without my having realized, without recognizing her. But when she went trotting by I somehow knew it was her, even if I was surprised that she looked younger than 40. Without thinking, I gave the horn an enthusiastic beep. She waved, but it was weird. I worried I'd made her uncomfortable. As soon as the security guards lifted the gate, I took off. I looked straight ahead, seeing the asphalt road and nothing else. I felt ashamed. I didn't turn or slow down or anything. Just the honk and straight home, a quick bite, then to bed.

Yogabriela: The kid listens to Metallica, wears black sunglasses, dresses all in black… he's a bad boy. Very, very bad. Bad bad. But he sees me and runs away scared.

Playmobil: First of all, it was Megadeth.

Yogabriela: Same difference. What's important is that I know your closet is full of black leather S&M clothes.

Playmobil: It's true. It was only by chance that you didn't catch me with a red ball gag in my mouth. And I didn't run away scared. Not even close.

Yogabriela. Hmmm. It seemed like you didn't like me.

Playmobil: What makes you say that?

Yogabriela: Because you barely even looked at me, and then you took off. Either way, I'm used to it. The same thing happens here with my husbaaaand.

Playmobil: No, I mean, why wouldn't I like you?

Yogabriela: Because I'm… a grown woman?

Playmobile: Okay, but you're hot.

Yogabriela: Finally you say something a little naughty.

Playmobil: It must be because I've been lonelier than Cobain lately.

Yogabriela: Let it all out! Nobody's judging you here.

Playmobil: Alright… TITS!

Yogabriela: Yes! There are so few daring men these days, and here I've got one between my tits.

Playmobil: Excuse me while I bungee jump into your cleavage real quick. I'll be right back.

Yogabriela: Go work up some courage. That way, the next time you see me you won't run away. Okay?

Playmobil: Run? No way. That's for old people who want to stay in shape.

Yogabriela: We stay in shape so somebody will want to touch the shape. Feel like it?

Playmobil: That's something that you don't talk about. You just go for it.

in my bed again
hundreds of spiders
hanging from the ceiling
fell onto me

.

i woke up agitated
went to the computer and looked it up
dreaming about spiders
it's a sign of prosperity and intelligence
but is also associated
with being manipulated
and may foretell
negative situations
that affect your
social
professional
and family environments
you don't say

After I quit studying, my parents stopped giving me extra money, and I refused to ask them for anything. So, without telling them, I quit going to the psychologist. The money they give me to pay her bill has turned into an allowance for their tormented son who pretends to continue treatment but actually buys beer and goes to the park with his friends from the old neighborhood. I'm sure you understand, Doc. It's not you, it's me, etc.

The whole time I've spent trapped in the country club I've wanted to live without needing money, but now I realize that everything costs something. It's bullshit. Having to earn money is the price of freedom. "If you don't study, you have to work." But I feel like I've made an authentic life decision. My parents want me to buy a suit and have responsibilities. There isn't time. It doesn't matter what I do or feel. They've never actually had any intention of making me learn the value of hard work and sacrifice. What's important is to keep me tied down to something so nobody thinks I'm lazy. That's what made me place the ad, which my mother's never acknowledged, in the newspaper.

Looking for work might seem like it would be easy for someone like me. Sure. When I was little, all the other kids could climb trees, but I never could. I didn't feel like it. They called me a fag and I got mad, but it still didn't motivate me to climb. Instead, I went home and cried into Lourdes's skirt, who caressed my hair and said, "It's okay, it's okay." Never in my life have I been able to fit in anywhere. I don't know how to make people like me. I don't even know how to play soccer.

Yesterday, the sound of the phone ringing woke me up. I answered, half asleep, thinking it might be Naty.

"I'm calling regarding your newspaper ad, sir," said a woman, and my eyes popped open. She was from an advertising agency. It was weird that she called me "sir." They wanted me to come in for an interview, to see if I fit the profile. I'd have to hide the reality of my life, but that was something I knew how to do

"I'm a marketing major," I lied. "I'm a sophomore."

I couldn't stop thinking about the call. Surely, it couldn't be that easy. There had to be some catch. Out of pure curiosity, I went to the interview in Puerto Madero. The agency is called "Happiness," and there's no sign on the building. A bald-headed security guard at the reception desk. He asked me my name and told me to go ahead. Mirrored elevator, fifth floor, white door with a bronze C on it.

A blond girl let me in. I didn't know whether or not it was appropriate to greet her with a kiss on the cheek. She made it easy by offering her cold hand. I was as nervous as if I had been trying to infiltrate the Russian mafia dressed as Ronald McDonald. The office occupies what used to be a big apartment. In a spacious living room, fewer than 10 people were doing something on computers. She took me to the boss's office. He was in his forties but acted like a kid. Button-up shirt, jeans, and sneakers. I walked in and he jumped to his feet.

"A pleasure to meet you," he said with a firm handshake. "I'm Tomás Alberti, the Managing Director of Happiness. Thank you, Flor. Come in. Sit down. First of all, I already know that you don't work in marketing. That's why you're here. It's obvious."

He talked quickly, smiling, and he didn't even look at the resumé that I'd worked so hard to fill with absurd lies and exaggerations, like saying I knew how to use the Microsoft Office suite. He offered me mineral water. He served himself and sat confidently in his high-backed chair. Behind him was a giant poster of Michael Jordan sticking his tongue out.

"Marketing is changing. Consumers aren't so naive anymore. They've grown incredulous. They see a guy on TV in black and white who used to have a sad life but is now happy and muscular because of some abdominal workout device he keeps under the bed, and they don't believe it. You know what I'm saying? My team can't be all publicists and ad people. We're going to revolutionize advertising here. We're going to drop a bomb. Understand? You have to hire people from other sectors." Without expression, he looked at my resumé. "You used to work answering the phone. You see? There it is. Customer service. That's worth something. You studied marketing. Fine. We hire sociologists, artists, photographers, clients, whatever you can think of. In this little world everyone claims to be a creative, but really they're very close-minded. Everybody's chasing a single dollar when they should be trying to make it rain dollars. I don't get tired of saying it: focus groups don't work anymore. They're little grubbing rat-people who come to get free stuff. They know the game. I don't trust them at all. It's time to *innovate*! Are you following me? We're going to use the internet to attack everyone. I'm looking for fresh faces that'll give me something new, and your ad in the paper absolutely killed me." He started laughing in short spasms, heh heh heh. He pointed to the wall where he had my ad pinned up with other papers and clipping. "Don't look at me that way. You know what I like? That you inserted some humor into looking for a job." I didn't understand anything. I didn't know what face to make. "We need humor here. Delirium. Something that breaks things up, like your ad. So many people who come here just go with the flow. I'm sick of seeing super cool hipster kids who say, 'yeah, exactly, totally,' all exactly the same, with the same haircut and the same glasses. That's why, when I read the newspaper, I noticed you. I promise I noticed you. I had a kind of vision. You can do well here. We need people to stir things up. Understand? People without a filter. Every idea can work." He gesticulated wildly the whole time. "I have a vision and I follow it. I like a woman? I go after her. That's how I've built this agency and my entire universe. And if I tell you that little by little you'll start to do well here..." He opened a drawer, took something out, and stood. "This is an idea. You see? This dart is an idea. Look, now you're starting to get it. Look, there goes the idea. It flies through the air and sticks in the bullseye." The dart was stuck in a blank space on the wall. "We're just starting to take off. We're a young company, and we have investment capital, right? There are important people who believe in us. Imagine it. There's a future here. But the most important thing is that we're going to shift the advertising paradigm, and with somebody else's money." He posed like he was a ship captain looking at the horizon. "Advertising isn't a mystery. We sell happiness, and everyone wants to be happy."

I agreed to work a six month trial period. I don't know if I'll be able to do everything that's asked of me, but it's a good way to get out of the country club. They'll let me know when my first day is. With any luck I'll be a sort of intern with pay and benefits, which doesn't seem so bad. For the first time in my life, I want to fit in. That's why I nodded along to everything he'd said. I even smiled. If there's one thing I've learned in life it's that, to do well, you have to give people the impression that you're obedient.

The
constant
struggle
struggle
struggle
of
having
to
interact
with
humans

.

Naty said she wanted to see me. "We need to talk," she wrote. Not just see me, but talk to me. We sat in my car so we could have some privacy.

"We're not okay. I need to be alone. I don't know what's up with me. I can't manage my time. I feel unstable. We see each other less and less, we don't call each other back... I don't miss you," she said, and she started to cry.

I hugged her, but she pushed me away. She wiped away her tears and stared at me. I felt like I had to break the silence.

"I don't understand. I don't get it," I said, even though I did understand and my chest hurt.

We didn't say goodbye. She got out of the car and ran away like she was escaping an attempted kidnapping. I stayed inside, not moving, a crash test dummy. I was conscious that I should cry, but I couldn't. I started the car. On the way home I rolled down the window so I could feel the wind on my face. I turned up my music. I didn't want to think. Nick Cave's *Murder Ballads* killed me too.

I floated in the pool like a dead man. Face down, not moving, like I learned as a kid, practicing holding my breath, counting the seconds on a stopwatch, trying to break my personal record. I'd looked from my bedroom window to see if the pool was clean. I even thought about jumping from there, but I didn't. When I got to the edge of the pool, I saw a bottle of wine and a glass on the other side, next to the trampoline. A flock of birds crossed the sky. In order not to make any noise, I got in the shallow end and walked toward the deeper part. Underwater, I screamed until I ran out of air. The bubbles tickled my face. When I surfaced, I didn't cry. I just felt my heartbeats pumping venom. I took another breath and floated like a dead man. Breathe as little as possible. Slow my heart rate and watch the seconds ticking on my Casio. I wanted to push myself to the limit or drown. Waterboard myself. Me against myself because I had destroyed the only pure relationship I'd been able to have in my whole life because I don't know how to say what I feel. I submerged myself, as if that would keep anything bad from happening.

I tested myself various times over the course of three hours and nobody thought I had died. Lourdes didn't even come out to the patio to pick up the bottle and glass. I could have stayed there until autumn came, until the water went swampy and leeches covered my body. The water turned black like oil when the sun went down. I felt my pruny hands and bit the flesh of my fingers. I got out. It had gotten cool like it was going to rain. I dried off a little and put on a t-shirt. I was starving.

I went inside, and there she was. Gabriela, in my house, dressed in some sort of Middle-Eastern mystic get up. She was like a woman Aladdin with the volume turned all the way up. My parents had invited her and her husband to dinner. It was high time to integrate into the little world of the country club, to socialize, to find another couple to be friends with, even if it meant exposing the truth of what our family really is. There was a high risk that, between comments about how delicious the sushi was, a wine glass would get knocked over and somebody would have to get blamed for it.

They talked about the vacation they were going on in a couple days. It was the first I'd heard of it. My mother thanked them for the tips they shared. "Thank you so much." "Oh, of course. Please." I went round and greeted everyone. I looked at my mother's face and there wasn't even a hint of anger, not for my ad in the newspaper, not because I'd come in the house with wet feet, for not having changed out of my wet shorts to eat, nothing. She was glowing.

"Come, sit here," she said. "Sit down."

I wasn't so sure. I didn't think I had any business being there. They weren't exactly the right crowd to talk to about how Naty had just broken up with me because she'd met a Maoist, but I took a seat. Lourdes poured me a Coca-Cola and, magically, she produced a ham and cheese sandwich from thin air. I don't like sushi.

Yogabriela said, "I see there's a little prince dining with us tonight."

Her cue-ball bald husband poured wine for himself. His round of chivalry started with Yogabriela. I watched her husband's manicured hand clutching the bottle, pouring. When the bottle approached my mother's glass, my father interrupted.

"No, thank you. She doesn't drink," he said, and he poured more water for her.

My mother flashed an impeccable smile and the husband nodded. He was about 50 or so, and he seemed too old for her, but this was because Yogabriela's life had come straight from a TV show or something. He was a bald ascetic from a Tool video who barely spoke, and when he did it was with great suspense, like Jack Palance. He's a classical pianist, and when I greeted him I felt like I'd invaded his personal space. He isn't one of those guys that greets men with a kiss on the cheek. I'm sure of it. Later, I looked him up on the internet. He isn't famous here. Only in Italy. It's his second home, he said. He doesn't like when people applaud during his concerts. Only at the end. In the interview, he said that his public knows that the music and its movements are structured from a lack of sound, that when a perfect silence comes over the auditorium, it's a musical whirlwind stronger than any applause.

We finished dinner and my father showed him the piano, but he gracefully declined to play. I went to the game room. A few minutes later, Yogabriela entered. The thin fabric of her dress outlined her body and made me feel somehow closer to her than if she were naked. Her hair was pulled back. I played pool.

"I got bored," she said. "Do you play piano too?"

"Nobody in this house plays piano."

"So why's there a piano in the living room?"

"I don't know. All I know is that nobody touches it."

"That's fortunate. Musicians are unbearable."

"Parents are unbearable."

"The bathroom?"

"It's over there." I pointed with the pool stick, and she walked over while I lined up the six ball with the pocket.

She was wiggling her ass for me. It was like I was aiming at her with the cue ball. Even though it was unnecessary for the shot, I hit the ball as hard as I could so she could hear how manly I was. The ball bounced around the felt, smashing into everything. I hit the wrong balls. The traitorous six didn't drop, and the carom sent the eight ball into the pocket. Even playing alone, I lost.

An embrace that erases everything we've said to each other.
An embrace that erases everything we've said to each.
An embrace that erases everything we've said to.
An embrace that erases everything we've said.
An embrace that erases everything we've.
An embrace that erases everything.
An embrace that erases.
An embrace that.
An embrace.
An.

I couldn't sleep all night. In an attempt to have trippy dreams, I tried listening to Mono, a Japanese instrumental band that Red had told me about. He'd said to put the volume low, and I'd be teleported in my sleep. I also tried some breathing exercises that the internet said were effective, but it was impossible. Then the sun rose. It wasn't anything special.

Lourdes knocked softly on the door. She knocked twice. Every other human on the planet is more frantic than Lourdes. A cuarteto song by the singer Rodrigo entered the room with her.

"Good morning," she said, optimistic. She told me about how my parents had already left for their trip, how my mother had called before their flight had taken off to make sure that everything was alright. They were on vacation in Miami. We were alone. She said she would stop by every other day. I told her I wanted to spend some time with Naty and that there wasn't any reason that anybody else needed to know about it. I felt bad lying to her, but she was so happy. I promised to behave myself and that we would talk on the phone whenever she wanted.

She sang in a low voice.

"Fue lo mejor del amor, lo que he vivido contigo. / Dejo mi esposa, tú dejas tu marido / para matarnos en un cuarto de hotel.[1]"

She straightened things in my room and picked my clothes up off the floor as she said that my mother had told her to give me her love.

"I don't believe you," I said.

---

1. Translation: "It was the best of love, what I've lived with you / I'll leave my wife, you leave your husband / so we can kill ourselves in a hotel room."

She hesitated, and a pair of socks fell off the mountain of clothes she was carrying.

"They came up early to say goodbye, but they didn't want to wake you."

Lourdes weaves threads of affection into every one of her actions, like she's trying to atone for some past sin.

When I was really little, before I was even four years old, a period that everyone claims to not remember, there was a birthday party in our house in Villa del Parque. I'm not sure if it was my birthday or whose, but there were a lot of people there, family members, friends of my father's, and other kids. What I do remember is being fascinated with a fire truck that Lourdes gave me and that I still have. That truck was one of the few things that survived that violent afternoon in which the other kids threw my toys onto the balcony and I smashed them with a baseball bat while wearing a Darth Vader helmet for protection. I remember a pirate ship exploding as a result of all my rage. Playmobiles rained down on the sidewalk.

Even now, it's not easy for me to be at an event like that. It was even worse when I was a kid. Everybody greeted me, and they expected me to do something amusing, something my parents might have taught me—give a cute little wave, make an angry face, sing a song I had learned in kindergarten, or do a popular dance.

Just like now, I went to my bedroom, and an unbearable, grating voice shouted after me. I didn't respond. Then I heard footsteps coming up behind me and there was a yank on my arm. I kicked and then limp-noodled while I was dragged across the living room to the table. In order to wrest my arm free, I struggled, and in the fight I knocked over a wine glass, which broke on the floor. The guests had averted their eyes, lighting cigarettes or looking away uncomfortably, but the sound of glass breaking drew everyone's attention. The puddle of wine spread over the beige tiles and I began to cry. One of my shouts turned into the word *mommaaa!*, which came out as I looked to Lourdes. I wasn't doing it with any sort of bad intention. Back then, I was a pure soul, full of life. Lourdes couldn't help but come to my rescue. She looked me over to see if I was hurt while simultaneously cleaning the spilled wine. Trying to separate us, my mother shoved Lourdes, sending her to the ground.

My mother waited for Lourdes to finish cleaning, telling me, as if she'd been the one I'd called out to, "You're okay. You're okay."

When the sound of silverware on plates started up again, my mother sat next to me. She poured herself a new glass and raised it to make a toast. Everybody else followed along, trying to pretend like nothing had happened.

After eating a bite of steak and taking another drink, she said, "I don't know why he's like this. I don't know where this craziness comes from. It must be because I didn't breastfeed him. I really don't know." She smiled politely, and the guests looked down at their plates while they ate. "And thank goodness. It turns your boobs into a horror show!"

I don't really understand where my mother had been before that birthday party. I spent the first years of my childhood with Lourdes. It's not hard to imagine alcohol and pills, but the only thing I know for sure was that she wasn't around. That's why, after dinner was over and everyone had gone, my mother called Lourdes down from the domestic staff quarters and yelled at her, insulting her, telling her that it was her fault I behaved so badly, that she should go back to her dirty house in the slums this very minute, that she didn't want to see her, that she could come back tomorrow to clean up the mess.

I ate lunch in bed: milanesas and mashed potatoes. Afterwards, I was able to sleep. I woke up at 6:00 PM. It was Sunday, and it felt like it. The first thing I did was look at my phone. Hopefully the agency calls me tomorrow and tells me to start working right away. There weren't any messages or missed calls. Nobody wanted to hear from me. I walked downstairs slowly. There was a low sound coming from the living room. I was wearing socks and didn't make any noise. Lourdes watched TV with the volume turned down. A news headline said, "CORRUPTION SCANDAL IN CONGRESS." She realized I was there, turned around, and, with a smile, asked me how I'd slept.

Flies
rub their hands together
because they know
we are factories
of garbage and decay
even
after
we're
dead

.

Walking toward the country club gates, I could just make out the devil horns on Mario's right hand, which he was holding out the window of Red's olive-green Taunus. The security guards hadn't let them in even though they'd given my address as their intended destination.

"The country club is pretty nice," said Mario. "The grass, the pool, everything. But the security guards have even darker skin than we do."

We were in my house, chilling. Mario poured fernet into the glass flower vase that my mom uses as a centerpiece for the table. The flowers were now decorating the trash can.

Red took the first swallow and asked when my parents were coming home.

"No idea."

"Great, then today we'll get fucked up and sleep over."

Mario said, "We could throw a party tonight."

I took a drink of fernet. For four in the afternoon, it was a pretty strong drink.

Splayed out on the living room couches, Red talked about how broke he was but how he wanted to take a trip to the United States to buy records and a Gibson. Impossible. Surely, he'd read in some music magazine from the record store that this is what musicians did. He'd been thinking about selling Marky Ramone's drumstick, the one he'd thrown into the crowd at the last show at the River Plate Stadium in '96. He said it made him sad to have to do it because the drumstick had searched him out.

He repeated, "It was the last show, man. The last show."

Mario's eyes popped open as if he had suddenly thought of a new way to make money without having to work.

"Remember when they did that promotional bottle cap thing and we smashed up all of downtown?"

I'd forgotten completely. The punks' vandalism revenge on Lavalle and Florida. Coca-Cola had come up with a promotion where you could trade in ten bottle caps for two tickets to the Ramones' last show, but, because thousands of people had shown up, they refused to honor the free tickets and all the Ramones fans destroyed the neighborhood. It was incredible. Mario said he had been there, but we didn't believe him. Since that day, every punk said they were there, kicking the capitalist system's ass.

"Maybe I'll post about it on some Ramones fan forum," said Red. I didn't think he could get very much for it probably.

It was pure gold to him. Along with the letter Nekro from Fun People had written back to him, it was his greatest treasure. He would never try to sell it. None of it was real. We were saying anything and everything, and it was beautiful. Mario said he would buy it for 100 pesos. Mario offers to buy everything for 100 pesos. That's his price.

It wasn't cold, but Mario lit the fireplace, just to play with fire. Watching the flames, an image of my father came into my head. It was from a few weeks ago. He had been burning papers. It hadn't been cold that day either. He was alone, after midnight, drinking whiskey and burning papers when he thought the rest of us were asleep. Red played "Stairway to Heaven" on the guitar, quietly, without singing. It felt as if I had invoked my father with the thought.

Mario said, "Your old man's job is nuts, right?" He was looking at the stone wall of the living room, the extravagant decorations, a statuette of an Indian. "Near my other grandma's house, my dad's mom, in Parque Patricios, there was a family that kidnapped, demanded ransom for, and killed businessmen in their basement." Mario spoke with a sense of captivating mystery. "They blocked the basement door with a wardrobe. It was across the street from the Huracán soccer field. My dad knew the guy. He seemed normal and proper except that he couldn't keep his mouth shut around women."

"Nothing makes sense," said Red, who seemed like he was in a trance, not listening to Mario, his fingers guided over the guitar strings by perfect inertia. Mario was gazing into the flames, possessed. He rapped, sang, and recited his lines, surfing over Jimmy Page's arpeggios as if he'd been born to improvise on a guitar or a machine gun. "In 94, they killed Cobain and cut off Diego Maradona's legs. Ever since that moment, nothing has made sense." Then he lit a cigarette and said that he would be good at covering up crimes, that he could hide anything.

He changed the subject.

"So, how's it going with Naty?"

Mario didn't let me answer.

"It's going bad. Can't you see how bad he's doing? You can see it in his face. Naty's gone, dude. It's done. Now that they're broken up, it's time to tell him, Red. Tell him. Do it. Don't be a pussy. Fine. Listen, Naty's not leaving you. She already left. She's with somebody else. Understand? You need to forget her. Burn it all and start over. On the phone you told me that you'd put all her gifts and photos in a box, right? Where's that box?"

All I could say was "That's enough, Mario." And for a moment I thought I'd stopped him.

But then Red stopped playing and said, "Mario's right."

With the letters, the teenage gifts, movie ticket stubs, a peacock feather, her sweater from that first night by the campfire, a silly straw in the shape of glasses you could wear and still sip drinks through, and a bunch of other stuff burning in the fireplace, within the cloud of the smell of burning plastic, Mario said, "It's fucked up, dude. It hurts, but I promise it's the only way. It's a ritual. Today, right here, tonight. Look into the flames and say goodbye. After my first girlfriend, I almost burned my grandma's whole house down because I didn't have a fireplace like this and I did it in a metal garbage can. Sabrina was a rock and roller." Mario took a long gulp of fernet, and a little ran down the side of his mouth. He wiped his face with his hand and said. "Man, I miss those rocker girls! Where are the rock and roll girls when we most need them?"

Red agreed. "Right?"

I took another slug of fernet and nodded.

Mario was just getting started.

"I miss those chicks with the hatchet-job bangs and torn up Rolling Stones t-shirts. I want a girl who drinks beer straight from the bottle, who bumps her ass into me while we're dancing at a show, kicking her white high-tops and leg warmers all over the place. Those asses can exorcize your demons, man. They have the power to get rid of the evil eye. Indigestion, too. Fucking nuts, man."

"Turn on the TV," said Red, finishing off the second flower vase, fed up because Mario wouldn't quit talking.

I turned on MTV.

"If you start watching TV, I'm out of here," said Mario. "I don't need them to tell me what to think."

They were playing an amazing video by a terrible and unmentionable band.

Mario was super drunk, acting like he was being interviewed in Rolling Stone.

"You know what the problem is? Every rock band is made up of rich kids. They're fancy boys who think they're rockers because they wear Ray Bans." His voice got sad. "I miss the VJ Ruth Infarinato. Where's Ruth Infarinato? Now that I'm older, I want to tell her that I'll love her forever with her bad attitude and sexy voice. Marry me, Ruth Infarinato! Let's have some little baby trolls with different colored hair, my love!"

We didn't throw a party.

"All the Country Club's resident owners must go to the chapel," Lourdes recited. Somebody had placed emphasis on these exact words, so she would know that she, and her Paraguayan face, were not welcome. I didn't say anything. I had smoked with the guys before they'd gone. I was watching TV and hating everything because sometimes I turned on the TV just to feel hateful. I am a larva.

I was intrigued, and I felt like at least seeing Yogabriela, even if there was only minimal contact, like the other night. It would help me continue on my quest to forget Naty. I put in eye drops and threw on my Yankees cap so I wouldn't have to comb my hair, and I went. In the country club's chapel, a line of people with worried faces whispered about what had happened. When I crossed the threshold and set foot on those tiles... silence. Everyone had gone quiet. I lifted my gaze to the walls to see a message written in capital letters and drippy red spray paint. THE GOD OF SUMMER. THE GOD OF SUMMER. THE GOD OF SUMMER. Over and over.

Up front, by the altar, there were three old ladies with white Italian porcelain teeth. Because of all the surgeries they'd had, they looked nearly identical. Just seeing them, I could feel myself aging. Medina accompanied them. I had heard of him, but I hadn't realized he looked so much like Sargeant Garcia in the *Zorro* television series from the '50s. He'd sweated through the armpits of his shirt. The old women held onto his arms. Even from where I stood, I could see how fake he was, and the look on the ladies' faces made it clear that they were gossiping. I surveyed the wall, looking over it from end to end, checking out every letter. I turned to my right and saw Him, the God of Summer. Somebody had put sunglasses on the crucified Jesus.

A few of my neighbors, accompanied by the security guards, came inside. They seemed embarrassed by the way their entrance looked, like they were VIP detainees. The priest, with a giant gold cross hanging around his neck, received them, waves of suspicion and blame pouring off of him. They lowered their gaze. There was a review of who was missing from each household. Some explained their reasons. Medina nodded as if forgiving them.

I looked for her everywhere. I even approached the altar. The faces of women trying to control their screaming children or stop them from running around the chapel. Their beautiful daughters with hair pulled back in fluorescent scrunchies. Alarmed faces. Yogabriela wasn't there. Nobody asked about my parents. Maybe they'd announced they were going to be taking a trip.

Only four or five people spoke. One of them was a slick guy, impeccably styled and with luminous teeth, dressed as though he was ready to play golf. He looked very alarmed.

"I don't think we're talking about isolated cases, here," he said. "And not a single cent has been stolen. We have to make important decisions. It's evident that we've become a target."

To calm everybody down, Medina's wife, who is the vice president of the Board and the First Lady of the country club and was dressed in the uniform of her position with a gold blond mane and face full of botox and worry, said, "I propose making a joint fundraising effort so that, in addition to our security here, the police can more carefully surveil the edges of the neighborhoods around our Country Club."

Most listened with attention and enthusiasm to her plan to obtain increased policing through subtle bribery.

Medina concluded the meeting by announcing that every aspect of security would be strengthened. He asked that the matter remain strictly confidential. Finally. Everybody's lunch had been delayed. The crowd started to stand, but someone interrupted, apologizing and stating that this time it would be important to avoid any and all media coverage. All eyes turned to Hubner, who owns the television channel that had broken the stories about government corruption and the previous robbery.

He carried his young daughter in his arms, and as he walked out he said, "I assure you, we won't be airing any dirty laundry."

What's
great
about nighttime
is
that some people
have the decency to
go to sleep
so
there are fewer of us
we're calmer
and
we get along
better

.

Yogabriela: You causing trouble again?
Playmobil: I don't know what you mean, officer.
Yogabriela: Hands against the wall.
Playmobil: Careful when you pat me down 'cause there's all sorts of stuff in my pockets.
Yogabriela: You know what the problem is? It's that the life of a woman police officer is awfully lonely.
Playmobil: Careful with that uniform. It's sexy, but it's intimidating too.
Yogabriela: I could take it off if you want…

After we finished chatting, all the while developing the storyline of the woman police officer and the detained vandal, both of whom ended up naked, the house phone rang. I didn't want to answer because I was hoping for Yogabriela to write another message. It rang again, and instead of continuing to stare at the screen, I picked it up.

The sound of her voice blew my mind.

"How are you?" I was speechless. She said, "What's up, kid? I'm at home, drinking caipirinhas.

"Hi," is all I could say. "What's up?"

"He went to Rome to play a few concerts. And I stayed home. I'm a very independent woman, aren't I? I didn't want to go." Her voice sounded strange, but she was in a fun mood. "I know you're all alone too. Don't tell me you're not. I saw Lourdes leave. I'm watching you."

Doorbell.

I jumped. I looked out the window but didn't see anyone.

"Hold on. Somebody's at the door," I said.

"Careful. Don't let anybody in," she said.

I walked downstairs barefoot, holding the cordless phone to my ear. I'm not a little kid, but the house is huge and I still get a little freaked out at night.

"If something bad happens, you're my witness," I said.

I looked through the peephole. It was Yogabriela. She wore a white shirt and jeans. She was smiling.

I opened the door and said, "Are you trying to kill me, or what?"

I was still holding the phone.

"Should we hang up?" she asked.

She was also wearing a striped necktie.

Sitting on the couch, with the TV on, I lit one to center myself a little. I smoked like nothing out of the ordinary was going on.

"This movie is dogshit," I said, without even knowing what movie it was.

With one hand, I flipped through the channels. With the other, I brought the joint to my lips. I passed it to her without asking if she wanted it. She laughed and took a tiny little drag.

"I haven't smoked for a long time." She asked me if I liked how her bangs had turned out. "I cut them myself before I came over," she said. She took the remote out of my hands. "Now who has the power?"

She took another puff and let the smoke out through her nose.

I took back control by climbing on top of her. I kissed her neck and then her mouth. I could taste the caipirinha's lime and the lingering flavor of the smoke. She kissed and bit my lips. She pulled away.

"Do you have any alcohol?"

"Yeah, fernet and beer."

"No whiskey?"

"I think there's some."

"Drink some whisky. Do it."

I poured one for myself, straight up, and I asked, "What's with the tie?"

"I thought it was appropriate for the occasion," she said. "Cheers."

I woke up early because I felt something poking into my neck. Her pearl earring had stuck into me. I got up and looked around for her, but she was gone. I looked out the window at her nice house, the tidy yard where bright flowers were planted between rocks. My head was killing me. Everything was foggy, and I wasn't sure exactly how things had gone down, but then I found her striped tie on the floor and I remembered how she had used it to blindfold me, then to tie my hands, then had asked me to choke her with it.

I took a look at myself in the bathroom mirror. I had dried blood on my neck. I washed my face. The doorbell rang and the sound of jangling keys came from downstairs. Lourdes was here. I moved the mouse to wake up the computer. I wanted to do a search to learn more about people who wanted to be choked when they were about to come.

A chat window flashed with a new message. It was Naty. "Are you there?"

But it was from earlier. She was offline.

Enough
!
psychology
protocol
and
good manners

.

Let's settle this
with fists
and lips
yin and yang
raw
let's go

.

I went to Villa Gesell with Mario. He said we were taking a weekend trip to the coast; he had to take care of a few things. He always needs to take care of a few things. Supposedly he needed my help. I never know what he's up to.

"I need you to drive me. I'll pay for gas and everything else. It's just one night. It won't be expensive. We've got a spot to sleep, and we'll come back early Sunday morning."

He acted like he was still trying to talk me into it, even when we were already on our way.

"It'll do you some good, man. You'll see. We'll meet a couple of girls and fall in love and end up living out there, in the woods, super chill."

We arrived Saturday afternoon. While he was taking care of things, I spent three hours waiting at a gas station on the edge of town. I drank six cups of coffee and read an entire newspaper. All bad news. Outside, trees swayed in the freezing wind. He came walking up fast, his hands in his pockets, his jean jacket pulled tight around him. We walked down Avenida 3 and entered an empty bar. The waiter didn't seem to feel like working. He didn't even seem to want to be alive. He hated us from the moment we walked in. Mario thought it was funny to keep making him get things for us. Another beer. More peanuts. More potato chips. Then he invited the waiter to have a drink with us, an offer that was declined. We ordered two ham-and-cheese sandwiches, another basket of chips, and we drank everything we could. We asked the waiter if he knew whether there was anywhere good to go out later.

"No idea."

We walked around, listening for any noise that might sound like it was coming from a party, but nothing was going on. The coast was dead outside of tourist season, ghostlike. There didn't seem to be anywhere to go to just be a friendly drunk. In the bone-chilling cold, we walked back to the gas station, and Mario asked the attendant if he knew what was up. He told us there was a brothel next door.

"That red door, right there," he said, nodding to it.

"Let's do it. Come on," Mario insisted.

"What are we going to do?"

"Come on, let's go. We still have to fall in love. What? You don't believe in love?"

We knocked, and they opened up without asking who was there. We walked up the stairs slowly, doing the best we could manage, given our state. I felt like it was better to take two steps at a time, supporting myself against the wall with my hands. A huge guy in a leather jacket met us at another door. While he patted us down, Mario talked to him like he'd known him his whole life.

"How's it going? Those are just my keys. All good. Whoops, *those* aren't my keys."

The silent bouncer opened the door.

Tambó Tambó was playing. Mario bellied up to the bar and ordered a drink.

"The cheapest whisky you have."

He smiled at the girls. One was barely moving to the rhythm of the cumbia.

He took little sips and said, "Let's seeeeeee here," but he took too long to decide anything and the girls got annoyed.

One girl, who had the Chacarita soccer club crest tattooed on her shoulder, told him she didn't have all night. Her hostile attitude drew him in like a magnet. He was sure that if he told her he was also a Chacarita fan, he might get a discount or something. He went with her while I sat on a tattered couch, drinking fernet, talking with a girl who slid her long red fingernails over my jacket.

She undid a button and said, "Aren't you hot, papi?"

When we left, Mario wouldn't let me get a word in edgewise.

"You bring me all the way to Gesell and you don't even take me to the beach," he said. You're trash. You're a piece of shit."

I had to follow him. Walking on the wet sand that clung to the inside of my legs, I told him that he had probably gotten an STD.

"I was too drunk to get it up," he confessed. "Can you believe it? Did you do it?"

"No."

"Why not?"

"I don't know. Not my thing."

"You weren't feeling it?" he asked sympathetically.

"No, I'm not into it."

"You're afraid."

"Yeah, absolutely. While I was waiting for you on the couch, the girl that unbuttoned my jacket started whispering in my ear like she was going to talk me into it, even though I'd already told her that I was just waiting for a friend. In between telling me what she was going to do to me, she said, 'I know your type well. You look like a goody-two-shoes.' Then, while she was playing with my zipper, she whispered in a low voice, 'Get me out of here. They have me locked up in here,' she repeated. 'They say that if I leave, they'll find me and kill me.' Suddenly, I wasn't just sitting on a couch grinning, I was scared for my life. And when I was just about to take off and leave you there, you showed up, scratching your balls and walking fast, like you'd read my mind."

We sat down. The sand's moisture entered my body through my ass. It was that specific kind of cold you only find on the coast. It helped me keep from vomiting.

"What are you doing?" Mario yelled.

He'd caught me sending a message to Naty.

He slapped the phone out of my hands.

He threw it in the ocean.

Without taking off my shoes, I ran into the water to search for it. I went in knee-deep and found it between waves. I pressed the buttons, but the screen was blank. I walked back to Mario, soaking wet.

"Quit writing her. You give in too easily."

He was writing his name in the sand with his foot.

When we got to the spot, we followed a hallway almost all the way to the back. It was fine. It seemed like a family home. I asked him how he had gotten the room, who it belonged to. He said he didn't know.

"Tell me, asshole."

"If I tell you, you're going to be annoying about it. Chill out and sleep."

I got into bed with my clothes on, only kicking off my shoes. I told myself there was nothing I could have done for the girl who had asked me to help her. The huge door guy would have kicked our asses, and the police, who were surely providing protection for the operation, would have burst in. Mario went into the bathroom. There was a long silence, but I couldn't sleep. I was drunk, and my head pulsed like the room was shrinking. I thought about the worst possible thing: what was Naty doing right now, tonight?

Mario came out of the bathroom, wearing the black transparent negligee that belonged to the prostitute Chacarita fan.

"Blowjob for fifteen pesos, handsome," he said in an exaggerated transvestite voice.

He'd stolen it when she'd gone to the bathroom, stuffed it down his pants and split as quick as he could.

I fell asleep without realizing it was happening, and when I woke up he was standing in front of the open fridge, drinking Coca-Cola out of the bottle.

He was still wearing the negligee.

They came back. One of their suitcases had been lost. My mother was on the phone, hysterically trying to track it down.

She said, "No, you listen to me, sir!" I imagined the way she must have covered the phone with her hand while she told my father, "Shut up. I don't have all the beautiful clothes I bought while we were there, and you can't get stuff like that here."

From the kitchen, he spoke up.

"I've told you a thousand times not to touch my stuff. You want to explain to me why you put my things in that suitcase, you idiot? I've told you millions of times not to touch my things."

When I walked into the living room, they were staring at each other with fury, and my mother changed the subject. I thought she was going to ask me if I had gotten a job yet, or how the search was going, but she only said, "How did everything go?"

It was a routine inquiry, satisfied with "Fine. All good."

My father continued digging through the other suitcases frantically, throwing clothes everywhere. I hadn't seen him so active in years. I left so they could have some alone time.

I didn't say anything about the agency, even though I'd been commuting to Puerto Madero for a week. I can't exactly say I'm "working" yet. I go to a place for eight hours, but I don't do anything. The biggest news is that I, a person who has been running late since the day I was born, haven't had any trouble getting up on time. Another benefit of having anxiety. Nevertheless, it takes more than an hour to get there, corralled in crawling traffic, moving toward a toll booth that charges you for the experience. That could dampen just about anyone's enthusiasm. Rush hour. A distraught woman insulted me because I didn't inch forward quickly enough. I was lost in my own world, listening to Radiohead's *The Bends*. Maybe singing and playing drums on the steering wheel weren't enough to get me through the drive to Buenos Aires anymore. Hatred for our fellow man is going to engulf us like a tsunami of shit.

I hurried out of the car because I was ten minutes late. A jogger taking his pitbull for a run nearly ran me over. Here, even the dogs work out. Entrance hall with bald security guard. He asked my name, told me to go ahead. Mirrored elevator, fifth floor, white door with the bronze letter C.

When I entered, there were only three people. Two janitors and the same receptionist.

"Welcome. I'm Florencia. Nice to meet you."

She didn't seem to remember me. She stuck out her hand. She didn't say anything else. The office was empty. Monitors showed screensavers of the word "Happiness" bouncing around. I hoped Florencia might tell me where to sit or something, but she was busy typing away on her computer. Every once in a while she smiled. She was probably chatting with someone.

I picked a random workspace and sat in it. I saw some whiteboards that had been written on with red, black, and green marker. Words in looping letters: branding, advertiser, dynamic rotation, etc. Geometric shapes had been drawn with almost perfect precision. There was a second person's handwriting. Unintelligible cursive. My coworkers started arriving about an hour later. They said good morning in a low voice. Three guys in their thirties, a woman older than 40, and a girl with very pretty green eyes who was probably about 20. When she came in, the room filled with the smell of her perfume. She chewed gum, wore a pink bracelet, and had her hair tied into a ponytail with a pink rubber band. She put on some pink and gray roller skates that she had brought in her backpack, and she started rolling back and forth, transporting papers and folders, as if she were organizing them. She was some kind of Cadet Barbie.

With every new person who walked in, I thought someone was going to tell me that I was in their space, but no. From their desks, they glanced at me discreetly and talked amongst themselves. Somebody turned on the TV. It was a rerun of *The Simpsons*, the one where Homer goes to New York to get his car back because Barney lost self-control the night he was supposed to be the designated driver. They didn't seem to have any idea who I was or what I was doing there. It occurred to me to ask Florencia if I could help her with something, just as a way to get a better idea of where to sit or what to do, or at least make time pass more quickly. I looked around, but didn't see her. A big guy with a viking beard, a Cannibal Corpse t-shirt, and a black suit jacket rushed in. The smell of coffee started to drift through the office.

Then a super skinny kid with short, straight hair came out of the kitchen and stood next to me.

"Hi. I'm Martín. You're in my spot." He smiled. "Want some coffee?"

Since then, every morning has pretty much been the same. Work is repetition. Until I was assigned a PC, I shared Martín's. It's painfully slow. Little by little, people started saying hello to me, everybody in their own style. The only person who I really talked to in those first days was Martín. One day he brought candies to share, but nobody paid much attention.

I've yet to be given a single assignment other than sitting next to Martín and watching him work. That's tricky because nobody really seems to do very much. It's like a simulation of work in which I try not to be noticed, though I'm not sure how long that can last. Most of the time, Martín, who I've started thinking of as "Friendly," sits in front of his computer, surfing the internet, chatting, or listening to music. I have to walk the line between being intrusive and seeming like I don't care at all. To talk about something, I asked if the agency was always so chill, practically silent. He told me that there had been weird vibes the past few months due to rumors of layoffs. The fact that I had been hired was a surprise. It had given everyone hope. What we ended up talking about most was music. He listened to Bowie, Beck, Morrisey, Luís Alberto Spinetta, Aterciopelados, Café Tacvba. On Friday, he put on "Dangerous" and started moonwalking in the middle of the office. Everyone else grinned and cheered him on. Another day, I confessed that I hadn't really listened to that much Bowie and that I thought that pop, somehow, had ruined everything.

"I'm going to pretend I didn't hear that. I'm going to make you a mixtape. You've got everything all wrong. You can't go on like this," he told me.

The director never came. I asked Friendly about him. He made a face and said, "That's just how it is here."

Male spiders are jealous. That's why, during sex, they tend to detach their reproductive organ inside the female, an act of self-castration so nobody else can penetrate her. They continue insemination, from afar.

After copulation, female spiders may eat the male in order to give strength and nourishment to their young.

A spider can lay thousands of eggs, and when they hatch, the babies eat the mother.

None of my attempts to contact Naty had received any response. I'd called her, sent her text messages, written her on chat. Nothing. I simultaneously love and hate her. I turned on the TV and in the Plaza de Mayo there were people protesting acts of corruption, the horrible economic situation, the congressmen and senators who were being investigated, and the widespread loss of jobs. Tons of people. The televised disaster surprised me. I never keep up with the news, and to see it all of the sudden was alarming.

"This puts the country's institutional stability to the test," said the worried-looking reporter. Then they cut to the live feed from Lanús where people had spent the past several hours looting. Immediately I thought of my father, maybe also watching TV, like I was, but feeling the fear inside, like a black ball, rock hard in the pit of his stomach, growing more and more abominable, wondering how much time he had left. The reports focused on the roadblocks, where exactly traffic was allowed to pass, and the fact that several people had been arrested.

I ran out to my car and turned on the stereo. The second verse of "Black Hole Sun" by Soundgarden played. For days, I'd had *Superunknown* in the car, playing on repeat like a never-ending album. When the song ended, I felt like I couldn't listen to anything else. I turned off the music. I was going to look for Naty. It was the only thing I could think to do, and I had grown accustomed to driving into the capital for work. I was scared for her. The images on TV had been charged with violence. I didn't know what I would say to her, but I knew I had to see her. Something would come to me in the moment.

Although it was also possible that I would just stand there with a dumb look on my face like, "what happened to us?"

I took the car in as close as I could, and I left it in a parking lot 15 blocks away. The attendant had a bad attitude.

"Seven o'clock sharp. It's going to get bad around here."

"Alright. I'll be here."

"Seven on the dot," he repeated, and I knew he didn't have any problem locking the gate and going home with my car still trapped inside the lot.

Approaching Plaza de Mayo, I walked quickly, like everyone else was doing, and I looked for Naty. I was searching her out like a third-world Terminator. In the distance were the sounds of drums, fireworks exploding in the sky, and people cheering. I looked and saw her everywhere, but it was never actually her. The plaza was full of flags. A rocket exploded 30 feet above my head, and I jumped. I kept going. There was a cordon of riot police with shields, a commotion of protestors, stones, and sticks. I heard shots, and the tear gas started to disperse the crowd. People ran by me, crashing into me, running again. I stood like a dumb mannequin, looking around, trying to take it in, scared and still searching for Naty. A disheveled guy with red wine spilled on his shirt fearlessly beat on a drum with a length of hose and shouted something I didn't understand but that ended with "sons of bitches." The guy looked at me, swaying, and he smiled with the few teeth he had left. He wasn't listening to whoever was yelling through the megaphone, but he seemed to be having a good time drunkenly shouting insults. I'd come to look for a girl. I didn't know which of us was more lost. A truck with water cannons drove in from the direction of the *Casa Rosada*[1]. People threw rocks and scurried in every direction. I joined the stampede, imitating those who covered their mouths and noses with their t-shirts, trying not to breathe the tear gas. The truck started spraying water, dyed sky blue like our flag. The police began clubbing whoever they could reach. Wom-

1. Literally "the Pink House," a palatial mansion where the president's offices are.

en, men, it didn't matter. In the distance, I saw a girl with short hair and a covered face. Something ignited inside me. Was it her? I ran towards her, tripping over thrown rocks and scraping up my hand on gravel and bits of broken stone, but I kept going. She'd just finished writing something on the asphalt in red spray paint, and she shouted from behind her red t-shirt. She turned toward me, but something exploded next to me and I ducked. My right ear rang. I closed my eyes and covered my head. When I looked up again, I could read her lips: "Are you alright?" I tried to stand, and for a moment I felt like I was going to faint. I faltered. She grabbed me by the arm and we walked quickly to the other side of the monument so I could catch my breath.

Agitated, she asked me, "Are you okay?" and I looked at her through the burning tears in my eyes to see if it was Naty.

It wasn't.

The agency director has started appearing occasionally, making charismatic entrances in which he confidently greets the whole staff before locking himself in his office.

"Florencia! Buy some sandwiches for everyone who's working so hard, please," he said once. Another time, he told her to go out for pastries, then he disappeared. Florencia quietly informed us that she wasn't going to buy anything. The last time she'd done so the boss hadn't paid her back.

I had my first work meeting. Except for the custodial crew, everybody was there. Project leaders, creatives, art directors, assistants, Cadet Barbie, and Florencia, who kept the minutes. The director was fired up, enjoying addressing his captive audience, putting on a show like a loud-speaking primetime host, talking about a car manufacturer, a soda company, and a stationery supply business that had now all placed their trust in us.

"They want to become millionaires, and they come to us because they know that here, with all these lunatics, if we wanted to, we could harvest the sweat from people at the gym, make a natural springwater juice with it, then we sell it back to them when they're done exercising."

In the afternoon, I had to stay late to pick up some print proofs and finish a Powerpoint.

When I was on my way out and didn't think there was anybody else there, he came out of his office and said, "Let's go, tiger. We'll pick it back up tomorrow."

We got in the elevator together. While he combed his hair in the mirror, I pressed the button for the first floor. He told me I seemed to be comfortably integrating into the team, and if I ever needed anything his door was open, etc.

In the street he asked, "How are you getting home? Want me to drop you off somewhere?"

I pointed to my car.

He looked at it and said, "One day you'll have one like this," and he pointed to his own, a brand new Audi parked behind mine.

"I don't know, this one takes me where I want to go and gets me to where I want to be. It's only problem is it's not self-driving," I said.

He waved curtly and got in his car. He didn't like that I had contradicted him. He shifted into drive and pulled into the street as I was still opening the door of my Peugeot 206. He honked the horn and accelerated away quickly. I've always wanted one of those horns that plays "La Cucaracha."

A couple days later, Florencia said, "He wants to see you," and I went to the director's office.

"Have a seat, have a seat. Want something to drink?"

"No thanks," I said.

He poured himself a glass of water and dropped an effervescent tablet into it.

Over the white noise of the bubbles, he told me, "I'll be brief. The other day, when we were leaving the office, you had an idea, but you didn't realize it." I had no clue what he was talking about. "Before we left, you said, 'It takes me where I want to go and gets me where I want to be. It's only problem is that it isn't self-driving. Well, there you have it. In that little detail, that touch of humor that's so you, the campaign for the car manufacturer we're working on is done. You see? It leaves an impression, right? Because a car should never leave you stranded. So listen. 'It takes me where I want to go. It gets me where I want to be.' Insert a little pause, and voilà. It's in the bag. Pure advertising. Ka-ching. You follow me? You have to listen carefully, pay more attention to what's going on around you. You have to steal subtly. We're thieves in white gloves. That's what it's all about. We're going to take your idea to the client. You're going to come to the meeting.

You're going to soak it in, and you're going to give the Powerpoint presentation. We'll make an advertiser out of you yet. And you'll start to realize how to butter the client up so at exactly the right moment you can deliver the finishing blow."

I didn't say anything, but I nodded to show that I understood, that I'd taken it in, and he ended the conversation.

"You're doing well. You don't realize it yet, but you're doing well. You'll see."

You
can't
buy
beers
and
fries
with
compliments

.

"Come in through the garage. I'll leave the door open," she texted me.

It was almost midnight, but I was nervous because my parents were still awake, watching TV in bed. I wrote out a response, but, before I could send it, I started to feel small. I went downstairs and paced around the living room impatiently. I went to the kitchen and drank a Coke. I wrote a new message, but I didn't send that one either. I went into the yard, shutting the door softly behind me. In Yogabriela's house, a strange, dim, orange glow filtered through the curtains, as if the lights were off and the house was slowly burning. From where I was, I could hear drifting hints of classical music. I sat in one of the patio chairs and waited for her to give me another signal, something to embolden me to sneak over to her house.

"Do it. Come over," she wrote.

I looked at the hedge and found a part that grew a little lower than the rest. If I went through the backyard, I thought I could pull it off.

I went upstairs and put on some black shorts, my black Pearl Jam t-shirt, a hoodie, and I committed. I took off running from the patio like a grunge ninja toward the low part in the bushes. It became immediately clear I couldn't jump over it, so I got down and found a hole that passed underneath, surely the same spot where the poodle without a collar that Lourdes had found a few times had gotten in. It was a small hole, but it kept me from having to climb over the hedge or do any other sorts of acrobatics I wasn't built for. Crawling, I made it to the other side in a few minutes. The bushes helped camouflage me in the dark so I could reach the garage door.

She was leaning on the hood of her red Volkswagen, waiting for me. She was dressed simply, wearing a white t-shirt printed with the words "All you need is love" and black leggings, as if she had just finished teaching a yoga class.

"The kid took his time."

"I was busy, Yoko."

"If you don't like the Beatles, you can go right back the way you came."

"The Beatles open every door in the universe, but what's up with that serial killer music?"

"Chopin calms me down, and it gives me a feeling of freedom. I don't know. Did you bring it?"

I took it from my pocket and acted like it was a lightsaber from Star Wars. Surprised, she laughed and snatched it from me.

She lit it with a barbecue lighter, gave a few puffs. Then she passed it to me and turned on a fan so the smoke would blow out the garage window. We smoked in silence for a few minutes. I couldn't think of anything to say, and she seemed comfortable enough. She looked at the sky through the little window, lit it again.

"Slow and steady," I said.

She didn't respond. Various tools hung on the garage wall. A sledgehammer, a saw, pliers, screwdrivers, a pressure washer on the ground. She held her finger to her lips, licked it, and pinched out the cherry. She opened the car door and took out a bottle of whiskey and a glass.

"Let's go inside," she said. "Come on."

We entered and the classical music intensified. The sound of piano music bounced off the walls and gave an epic quality to every step we took up the stairs. On the landing, she spun around and kissed me and squeezed my ass in both hands.

"You're cute with your hair all messed up like that," she whispered.

She knelt down, set the glass on the ground, and lifted my shirt to start kissing my stomach. I felt the hairs on the back of my neck stand up. She slid down my shorts and started licking slowly, without using her hands, looking straight into my eyes. It felt weird, there on the stair landing, but I was into it. She handed me the whiskey glass. I drank from it while she, little by little, lick by lick, gave me a very serious erection. She took the glass back from me and drained it while she worked furiously with the other hand. I buried my hands in her hair and pulled her toward me. She started slowly, but deep. The piano was crazy. Her eyes were lit up wildly. She was still looking at me, and the whiskey had turned her mouth into a wet fire, sexual lava, and I held myself up against the wall. She kept sucking and stuck her fingers into my mouth. I was almost there. The fiery swirls continued until my knees went weak and I moaned and bit down on her hand.

Sitting on the landing, she took another drink and said, "I covered your mouth because he might have heard us," and she nodded toward the living room. A violent piano crescendo flooded the house.

I started going out for lunch with Friendly every day, maybe infecting him with a little bit of the hate I have for my fellow man. We stopped eating at the office, stopped trying to integrate ourselves into that group of beautiful humans. He continued passing out coffee and promoting kindness, but at midday we went for walks. We'd buy two hot dogs and a soda and sit on a bench in the plaza three blocks from the agency. An escape.

During the past month or so, Cadet Barbie has joined us a few times. She's nice, and she and Friendly have good rapport. Ever since I first met her, she's given me the impression that she gets along better with men than she does with women. She can drink a beer and eat a hotdog in the plaza without sacrificing any sense of delicacy. She tears the hotdog in two and eats it like it's a cocktail canapé.

We discussed trivialities, for example how strange I find people who don't put condiments on their hot dogs, like Friendly. Or people who don't like chocolate or dulce de leche. He talked about how to spot weirdos. We identified the weirdness in everyone, taking our own little tour of the office gossip. The problem that Florencia the secretary had created by having sex with two different colleagues, who now had to see each other every day while the rest of the office commented. The guy who had a pet ferret. The bald 26-year old whose hair implants didn't quite grow in all the way. The guy everyone said was a swinger because his wife had too much champagne and hit on Florencia in the bathroom at the Christmas party last year. The director's pectoral implants. The lonely lady who thought a long-lost former schoolmate had come to see her and ran out the front door and straight into the police, who had come to repossess the car she hadn't been making payments on. Every time we named someone he didn't like, Friendly said, "That asshole's going to heaven," or "She's going to heaven for sure, the bitch."

One day when Friendly and I were alone, we got high and tried to think of ways to completely blow the minds of stereotypical housewives in order to sell them cleaning supplies. I asked what Cadet Barbie's deal was. What exactly went on under the pink exterior of headphones, photocopies, complaints about the perpetual lack of printer toner, and the way she zigzagged on roller skates while delivering documents? I was pretty sure there was something going on between Barbie and Friendly, but it hadn't made it to the gossip list.

"Not at all," he told me. "She's a super special girl, and I even think she's hot, but I'm not into girls."

The sentence swung at my head like an ax. *Chunk.* He hadn't even hesitated for a second. He'd just said it. I wasn't a stranger, but eating lunch together didn't necessarily mean we had that level of trust. He'd told me like he was saying "good morning." My dumb head thought that it might have been an attempt at picking me up, that he had been so friendly to me because he wanted to show me his Michael Jackson moves. In his apartment. Naked. My face must have communicated as much.

"Don't flatter yourself," he said. "I don't like straight guys either."

As we were finishing the joint, I tried to steer the conversation back to the workplace. Before we knew what was happening, there was a guy standing right next to us. He'd come from the part of the plaza we had our backs to. Friendly became immediately confrontational.

He stood up and said in an aggressive voice, "What's up, huh?"

The guy opened his denim jacket. But he didn't pull out a gun. It was a police badge.

We looked behind us and saw his partner speaking into a walkie talkie. Two plainclothes cops. I couldn't believe it. I worried I might still have something incriminating in my pocket, in addition to what we had just been smoking. But I didn't.

"Where are you from?" the cop asked.

I had flicked the roach under the bench, but the smell of smoke still hung in the air.

When they searched us, it turned out Friendly had a little bit stashed in his underwear.

They started squeezing his testicles, and he yelled, pissed off, "Get the fuck out of there you fucking faggot son of a whore." That's when everything went to shit. "That make you hard, you corrupt piece of shit? You going to arrest me for smoking in a plaza? Go get some actual bad guys," he yelled.

The cops tightened their hold, and my right cheek slammed into the plaza's cobblestone pavement.

Friendly changed his tone and started trying to negotiate.

"Between us we've got at least 300 pesos. Go ahead. Let's make a deal, and you'll never see us around here again," he said while I watched cars drive past in the avenue. People walking by looked over and quickened their pace.

All the corrupt cops in Buenos Aires, and we had gotten a couple of real heroes.

As they loaded us into the wagon, I couldn't help myself. I asked why they were arresting me if I didn't have anything illegal on me. But it was obvious that things weren't going to go our way.

"We're arresting you for being a dumbass."

Locked up. While I was getting a grasp on what this meant, Friendly was fuming. I tried to talk to the guard, telling him they couldn't put us away for smoking, that we worked in the advertising agency that was right around the corner from the station, Happiness.

Friendly exploded.

"What are you saying? Don't talk to him! I'm gonna piss all over your police station, pig!" he yelled. "And you're going to have to clean it up. That's what you get for not studying in school."

I was worried that the guard would come in and club us, but nothing happened.

A few hours later, Friendly finally got tired, and the idiot fell asleep sitting on the floor. That's when the director appeared. We'd left work at one, and now it was nearly nine. He bailed us out and told us he'd drive us back. I felt ashamed the whole way. We didn't talk. He put on electronic music, turned down low.

When we got to the office, he spoke.

"Good thing you told them you work at the agency. The chief is a friend. Now go home. I didn't mention anything to anyone and nobody called looking for you."

In São Paulo, a group of patients with arachnophobia were cured using therapy that consisted of showing them a series of images. Photos of tripods, a carousel, dreadlocks, and other objects that became more and more arachnid-like without ever actually being spiders. Last night, I knew everything that was going to happen in my dream, but I still woke up sweating.

I didn't pick up. I left my phone on silent and watched Yogabriela's name blink on the screen. Not only did she call and text constantly, telling me every little thing that happened to her, but one afternoon I came home to find her drinking tea with my mom, who was saying, "Just a little lipo, Gaby, a tiny refresher like that can change your life." Since my parents had gotten back from their trip, my mom and Yogabriela had been spending more time talking. Their relationship had grown stronger.

I greeted Yogabriela in a friendly way. I didn't do so much as wink at her—nothing of the sort. My brain was fried from everything that had been happening. Plus, I couldn't deny that Yogabriela's insistent communication had left me feeling overwhelmed. The intrusiveness was such that I'd come home one night to find a new shirt gift wrapped and placed on my bed. I'd thought my mom had bought it for me, and I tried it on. As I was doing so, a text message arrived: "How does it fit, kid?"

I kissed Yogabriela on the cheek, and she said, "Ooh, very nice cologne. What a handsome young man. Something's been going on with him lately, right? He must have a new girlfriend or something." She was trying to pump my mom for information.

My mom said, "She told me that you've been asking her for yoga tips, as a way to destress after work. Is that true?"

I forced a smile and nodded. She said how happy she was about my lifestyle, that I was finally taking care of myself and my body.

Yogabriela looked me up and down. The way she'd been

talking in innuendos, even in the presence of my mother, made me feel trapped.

That's why, later, I didn't pick up.

She kept calling and leaving voice messages.

"Hi, baby. Answer my calls. I need you to come over. Just a little kiss."

"It's me again. Alright, I see you're busy."

In another, after a long and uncomfortable silence, she coughed and said, "Please, I'm asking you to come over. I swear I'm alone."

"Hello…" then she called me a bad name and hung up.

"I'm sorry, baby. I didn't think it would bother you so much."

Crying this time: "I can't understand you. I wouldn't call if it wasn't important. I'm unbearable. Please forgive me, but I need you to come to my house. I'm not okay. This is humiliating."

The last message was what finally made me go. I figured we would actually be alone this time, but, just to be safe, I paid close attention to my surroundings and peeked through the living room windows before knocking. It was the first time I had ever gone to the front door. No answer. I tried the doorknob. The door swung open. The living room and the study were perfectly organized, as if they had just been photographed for a feature in an architecture magazine. Through the open window, I looked out at the quiet park. I went upstairs and called out for her as I walked down the hallway. I reached her bedroom and looked inside cautiously. The bed unmade, the TV turned on. At the end of the hallway, the bathroom door was closed. I knocked slowly. Knocked again. Nothing. I tried to open the door, putting my weight against it, but it didn't budge.

I shouted, "Gabriela!"

There was no answer, and I started to panic. I checked her bedroom again, the hallway. I discovered another doorway that led to the upper part of the house because a gust of wind made it slam shut and I just about had a heart attack.

I climbed the stairs that led to the rooftop terrace. Laundry on the clothesline—the whites—fluttered in the wind. Two legs poked out from beneath the clothes. She was barefoot, her toenails painted black. She wore only her panties and a white t-shirt that left the bottom of her buttcheeks exposed. She was holding a glass of whiskey and her hair was windblown and crazy.

When she saw me, she said, "Hi, cutie. You want some?"

"No thanks," I said. "What's going on?"

She spoke as if we'd already been talking for hours.

"You have no idea what my life was like before. Look at everything I have now. Look." She sipped her drink and contemplated the view from the rooftop. She swallowed and made a face. Her hand was trembling. "Not in my wildest dreams did I think I would be somewhere like this. And now I feel like I truly deserve it. But my mom calls. Every morning my phone rings, and I know it's her, and she asks me how I am. I tell her that I'm fine, but I don't really know. I'm whatever. I'm alive, which isn't nothing. But I can't figure out if I'm actually okay. I can't deny that I have a good life. I have everything I want. Not only what I need, but what I want. Hundreds of purses and pairs of shoes. I have a workout room. I have an indoor jacuzzi and another one in the backyard, next to the pool." Lightning flashed overhead. "And then you showed up, and now you're going to have to go away. As difficult as it is, we can't go on like this. Do you understand?"

I nodded, agreeing without fully understanding. Chatting night after night had gotten me thinking, but only until I'd come. Then, after having sex with her, the platonic nature of our relationship had disappeared. It had taken me to the edge of something new, but I'd immediately seen the way her personality changed as a result, and I'd started to take some space. She spoke to me as if I were about to tell her that we should run away together, start driving and see where we ended up, listen to Aerosmith's slow songs and hold hands over the stickshift.

Every few minutes, she said, "These might be my problems, not yours."

We didn't say anything for a while. She sipped whiskey. She kept offering it to me, and I kept declining. With the sky staring down on us, we looked out at nothing, listening to the country club's limited soundscape. Down the block, a mother called her children inside. The first drops had started to fall. Then a clap of thunder split the sky and a swirling storm broke loose, sending rain pouring down. We took down the laundry and laid it out in the living room, spread over the table and chairs. I wanted to leave. I was soaked after even just a few seconds in the rain. She'd gone into the kitchen. There was no reason for me to be there.

"I'm going to take off," I said from the living room.

"Alright. Thanks," she responded, staying in the kitchen.

I heard a noise at the front door. Yogabriela's husband came running in, closing his umbrella. He's a big guy. I imagined him stabbing me in the stomach with the umbrella, killing me.

"My god, what a storm," he said. "Good evening." He wiped his hand on his pants and reached out to shake mine. "You doing good?" he asked.

"Fine, thanks," I said.

I was on the front steps, psyching myself up to run home, when I heard him call out, "Honey, I'm home!"

I dreamt
about spiders
but during the day

.

I fell asleep
on
the
couch

.

In
the
dream
it
was
nighttime

.

The embarrassment I felt around the director didn't last long. It helped that he hardly ever came to work in the days that followed. He was always leaving for somewhere else. Friendly and I stopped going to eat in the plaza, instead choosing to use the agency's shared break room. We made sure nobody found out about anything, except Cadet Barbie. Our plan was to tell her the story as a way to find out if she'd already heard it, but halfway through we realized that what we'd really needed was to have someone to talk about the experience with. We interrupted and talked over each other, describing the event in vivid detail.

"I can't believe I missed it," she said, laughing. "I'll never forgive you for leaving me out."

Something changed after that. The three of us started seeing each other differently. And Friendly pointed out that Barbie was looking at me in a new, special way. I told him not to fuck with me, but I could feel something growing inside me, a sick curiosity. Could those pink lips and roller skates be my Courtney Love?

I tried to do whatever the agency asked of me, but I couldn't manage much productivity. I was too busy studying Cadet Barbie, an activity that felt like giving little bits of cheese to my inner rat. I'd thought she was beautiful before, but now I longed to touch Belén's bare skin. Cadet Barbie's name was Belén. She used bubblegum-scented makeup that made me want to lick her face. But, because she was a nuclear reactor of good vibes, I worried she'd plunge the dagger of "friendship" into my heart, all while flashing that explosive smile.

I was starting to like her so much that I needed to call Red and tell him about it. Florencia, the secretary, made calls all the time, out in the open. Finally overcoming the lingering fear and trauma instilled in me by the concentration camp call center, I went for it. Nobody cared. It helped that the TV news was turned up loud, playing the corruption trials and hidden-camera investigative stories, like a political reality show. I wanted Red to give me some advice about how to get with Belén, but instead he told me he had formed a band. He didn't care about anything I had just shared with him.

"We practice three times a week. You've got to come and hear us. You can't imagine how good of a singer Mario is. And we found a good drummer. He plays fast and almost never says a word. His dad is a record collector who comes to the shop looking for rare pressings of Yes or Rush, all prog stuff. I put up a flier, and he showed up the next day with a beautiful maple drum kit." Red couldn't stop talking. "And you know the bassist. Remember Esteban?" I didn't. "The dude from junior year who had long hair and played the guitar and was super annoying? Whatever, it doesn't matter. Mario ran into him in the street and told him we were looking for a bassist so we could record our first album and shine a spotlight on Argentine punk. He's come to one practice. He plays well, really well for a bass player. But I'm not giving up my position as guitarist, I don't care how long his hair is. Anyway, we were practicing, and we finally decided to play a show. We're playing tomorrow."

"Tomorrow?"

"Yeah. We didn't tell you about it because we didn't want to talk all big and then end up sucking, but whatever. Tomorrow we're going on stage. We have four original songs, and then we'll play some covers. I can't say too much, but Mario and I have chosen some serious gems. They sound pretty good at practice. You know what Mario told me when I told him about the show? He said, 'We're going to bring punk back to life with an electric shock to the balls. I'll cut myself on stage, I don't give a fuck.'"

Red's imitation of Mario was perfect, and it cracked me up. While he was talking to me, I couldn't shake the feeling of déjà vu. Just as I was about to congratulate him, I saw my dad's face on the television. Front and center. The title read, "Power's Proxies." I looked around to see if anyone recognized my last name on the screen. Nothing. It wasn't like I had that unique of a last name, anyway. I told Red to hang on a sec. On hidden camera, my father's weasel face. Then a shot of the inauguration of a project in Río Turbio, men in suits standing around him, people applauding. Then they reported everything my father owned: an apartment in Miami, a yacht in Delta, a private plane, accounts both offshore and in Argentina, and the house. "Money laundering," they repeated. A helicopter shot zooming in on the country club, of which he was also apparently the majority shareholder. The truck parked in the driveway, the pool, my mom sunbathing in a lounge chair. Naty in her bikini, swimming with me that day in summer. They talked about the brief amount of time in which he had been able to amass his fortune, and they showed an infographic with all the businesses that were registered under my father's name.

"There's Happiness," said the guy with the pet ferret, pointing at the TV.

I hung up on Red without saying goodbye.

I looked toward the director's office. He wasn't there. I broke out in a cold sweat.

Friendly asked me if something was wrong. I told him no, that I'd just found out my friends had started a band.

"When are they playing?" he asked.

"Tomorrow?"

"Let's go."

"I'll let you know. I'll text you."

"There's fresh coffee," he said.

I shook my head. I was still putting the pieces together. I was working for my father. That's why my mother had never reacted to the ad I'd put in the paper. Without having realized, that was the moment I'd fallen into their web. I sat there silently, like a little bug that didn't know how to escape.

I collapsed.

The idea that I could manage my own life, that I could get a job without having to rely on anyone else. The pride I felt every time I got a paycheck or the director complimented me for what were supposedly good ideas. Those things have all come tumbling down on top of me. I thought I was good at something. This time, I really thought I was special. But it's all been a farce. The lie feels like a bad joke. Disappointment and humiliation turned my mouth sour.

This was the last night. The last night I would have this unbearable lump in my throat. Words came into my head like a whirlwind. Thinking clearly was impossible. I walked around the country club, wondering why everything had changed so much, why my father wanted to drag me through the mud with him, to make me his puppet. I was a puppet's puppet. I took off my shoes and walked barefoot. The sprinklers were on, and my feet sank into the spongy soil and wet grass.

"Identify yourself!" somebody shouted from behind. I turned, blinded by bright flashlights the size of motorcycle headlamps. I shielded my eyes and could see two figures about 30 feet away. "Security! Identify yourself!

I couldn't tell if they were pointing anything other than flashlights at me. I told them my name and my address. I put my hands up in an unconscious reaction, and they were quiet. They lowered their lights and walked toward me slowly.

"So sorry we had to shine our lights on you like that. We didn't recognize you."

"I couldn't sleep. I thought I might go for a walk. It was a bad idea."

A pause.

"We'll take you home," one of them said, trying to sound friendly. It looked like he had just gotten a haircut.

"That won't be necessary."

They drove me home in their little golf cart. I'd left my shoes behind.

On the way home, one of the security guards, suddenly becoming overly outgoing, opened up.

"Residents reported prowlers in the night. Surely, they did it so we would be a little more attentive because — well, you know why. But it's as quiet as a church out here."

The other one stared at him, trying to get him to shut up.

I walked inside, eyes unfocused. My mother was falling asleep in front of the TV in the living room. The cable news repeated the story of the corruption scandal. Now they were saying something about drug trafficking as well. It was a national outrage. Again, they showed my father's face, caught on the hidden camera. On the coffee table were a wine glass and a bottle. She jumped when she saw me. She tried to take another sip but realized there was nothing left.

"I thought you were your father," she said through wine-stained lips. "They delivered that fucking lost suitcase today." She slurred her words.

I started packing up some of my things. Shoes. My computer went in my backpack. A silent scream of hatred burned in my chest again, driving me to grab things at random. Tissues, clothes, cold medicine, my ID, a few CDs, a jacket, a pair of dice, and my guitar.

I left a handwritten letter for her, as though writing everything down would open the door for me to leave. I needed to tell my mom what I felt: "It's too late to air grievances. I don't know what happened, but here we are. This is what we are. I hope you leave too. I'll be fine. XOXO."

I got into the car and rolled down the window, feeling like I couldn't breathe. In the garage I saw the returned suitcase that had been lost. It was waiting for my father. Who knew if he would ever come home. I got out, picked it up, and put it on the passenger seat. I pressed the button on the garage door opener. The door raised slowly, revealing Lourdes's legs and torso as though she were a ghost sweeping the driveway. She stepped aside so I could pull out, and she nodded to me. She was crying. I pulled away quickly. Just outside the country club, there was a van with a TV station logo on its doors.

I called Mario, thinking he would still be awake, but I woke him up. I told him I needed to stay at his house for a couple days. In a gravelly voice, he told me that was fine. It was the only place where anybody who might want to find me wouldn't be able to. I sent a message to Red as well. Mario opened the door in his boxer shorts. He didn't ask me anything. We didn't bump fists. He gave me a hug.

"Make yourself comfortable over there," he said, and he fell back into bed.

The house was a wreck. Broken glasses made into flower vases. Pothos vines everywhere, even in the bathroom. Mario had the ability to keep things alive in his house.

I'd forgotten about the next day's gig. It wasn't exactly the best day to go out in public, but Friendly had just written me back about going to the show: "I invited Belén to see your friends' shitty punk band and she said yes, that she'd love to. I'm sure it doesn't have anything to do with her maybe liking you."

RAMON, the punk club, wasn't open yet. It was six in the evening and heat bounced off the asphalt, pushing up into my body through the soles of my sneakers. I pounded on the metal grate that covered the venue's door.

From inside, a woman's voice shouted, "What?"

I would have said I was a member of Red and Mario's band, but I didn't know what they were called.

"I'm playing here tonight," I said. I thought that might get her to let me in.

A skeletal woman opened the door. The smell that wafted out told me she was smoking Parisiennes cigarettes. She wore an Iron Maiden t-shirt. No bra. The sound check was going on. I walked in without having to answer any more questions. With the lights off, like they usually were, the club was a complete mess. When the lights were turned on, like they were now, it was even worse. The only reason there weren't vermin was because it was too gross for rats, even. The musicians were on stage. Below, two girls watched them, one dark, the other blond with a nose piercing. Seeming to move in slow motion, the skeletal woman and the bartender wiped down the tables with disease-ridden rags. A 14-inch television hung over the bar. The image was sort of green-ish. Everything might be falling apart, but tonight was about punk rock. I was surprised how tight the band sounded given that they hadn't been playing together very long.

Red saw me and stepped up to the microphone: "Boogeyman's in the house."

They came down from the stage, and Red introduced me to the drummer, who was growing out his mohawk. The bassist had gone to the same high school we had. That piece of information didn't generate even the slightest enthusiasm in any of us. In front of the other guys, Red asked me what I'd thought. I told him they sounded like a train full of passengers barreling straight at you. The bassist and drummer went to hang out with their girlfriends, and Red and I ordered beers. In a low voice, he told me he had no idea where Mario was.

"He got here first and was hanging out with the other bands, but then he disappeared. I lied and told the other guys he went to look for someone," he said. "I'd prefer to be the only one freaking out."

The bathroom looked like Chernobyl. Above the urinals, at face-height, a sheet of paper was taped to the wall. Handwritten on it were the names of the bands that were going to play: Bad Milk, All Your Fault, Nasal Hemorrhage (La Plata), NO NAME, and Pogo Death. The guys were going on second.

Pogo Death had already started and were butchering a cover of Green Day's "American Idiot" while four punks did a sterile pogo in front of them. I thought Mario would come back right then, drawn by a desire to kill them. From across the room, I saw Friendly and Belén arrive. She was laughing and playfully punching him in the shoulder. I could read Friendly's lips: "Stop it, freak." I said hi, and we went to the bar. With disdain, the bartender turned off the TV. I ordered three beers and the band announced their last song.

"Cheers to that."

Belén wore a gray t-shirt featuring Jimmy Hendrix in front of black, yellow, green, and pink psychedelic waves. From where I stood, her face blocked my view of the band.

"Stay right there," I said. "Now put up your index fingers."

She looked at me, surprised. I grabbed hold of her fingers and stuck them in my ears.

She laughed and made a disgusted face—grossed out by my ear wax—and I fought the urge to put her fingers in my mouth. We listened to the rest of their last song, which was an original and wasn't so bad. I didn't know how to break the news that I wasn't ever going back to work at the agency. It wasn't the right moment. There would be time to tell them later.

While Pogo Death broke down their gear, Red discretely called me over to where he was tuning his guitar. There was still no sign of Mario, and they were supposed to go on in five minutes. I tried to calm him, then I sprang into action. I went to the door. He wasn't out front. I walked quickly around the block. I figured that if Mario was anywhere, he was probably in the street.

On the corner, some guys were drinking bottles of beer. A scrapper came by with his family, pulling a cart full of re-cyclables. On the cart was an old television. My phone rang, but I didn't answer. When I had made it almost all the way around the block, I heard music from the venue and I started running. I figured they'd decided to play anyway. When I got inside, I saw Mario jumping up and down on stage.

He was wearing a policeman's hat and frantically shaking the microphone, yelling, "We're all gonna die / We're all gon-na die / Give me you're stubborn mouth, baby / I'm looking for something to kill me / You got no place to escape to / You got no place to go to."

I went back to the spot by the bar, where Belén was nod-ding along to the song. She gave me a thumbs up. The guitar riff blasted through my skull, and Red hammered away at top speed, like there wasn't time left for anything, like the world was going to end at any second. The drummer was pour-ing sweat, and it was only the first song. The bassist stared straight at his girlfriend with the nose piercing. It was obvi-ous that every note he played was dedicated to her. She might as well have been the only person in the club. Mario bit his lips, stuck out his tongue, and marched around like a soldier. There was some feedback from the PA, then Mario roared like a three-headed dragon spitting fire.

Now the show had really gotten going. The 40-or-so peo-ple in the crowd didn't know if they loved Mario or if they hated him, but they knew something interesting was happening. The parents of one of the other musicians, standing in the back and waiting for their kid's band to play, looked offended. I went to the bar, and the bartender, who had seen the very worst bands in the world, was watching attentively.

I came back with three beers.

About Mario, Friendly said, "He's got an Iggy Pop thing going on, or maybe more of a Borda psychiatric hospital thing. What does he have written on his chest?"

It said, "Break glass in case of emergency," and there was an arrow pointing to his heart. They had started playing "Runaway."

Mario looked strange to me. His energy had dropped since the last song. Maybe he didn't like playing a cover, even if it was a song by Fun People. First he stood next to the drummer, then he walked around the stage looking lost, singing without any heart. I wondered if I was the only one who noticed, or if I was wrong and it was just part of the show.

The song ended. We all clapped.

Red said, "We don't have a name yet, but we have this song. It's called 'Cannibal Scream.'"

The bassist and drummer started a slow beat. Mario spat on the floor, stood next to Red, and yelled something in his ear, practically falling on top of him. He gave him a strange look then smiled. The bassist was still making the most of every moment, staring at his girlfriend with the piercing.

I stood close to Belén and said, "I'm glad you came."

She spun around quickly, like my lips next to her ears had tickled her or made her shiver. We were face to face, staring at each other. I leaned in a little bit so I could kiss her. Then I heard the amplified thud of the bass hitting the ground. The crowd jumped, startled. The pierced girlfriend screamed. Belén pulled away from me and raised her eyebrows in surprise. Another girl said that Mario had punched the dude in the face. The bassist fell off the stage, blood pouring from his nose. Mario panted like an animal.

The set was over. While the next band set up, I tried to keep everybody calm. The bassist had to be taken to the hospital, and Mario cried backstage. I'd never seen him cry.

Red said, "I knew I fucking recognized her."

Suddenly, it dawned on me that the bassist's girlfriend, the girl in the crowd with the piercing, was Andrea Di Marco, the girl that Mario had been crazy for in high school. He'd written her letters and pursued her as best he could, in his own Mario way, until she slapped him in front of everybody at the end-of-year dance, and he dropped out. From that day on, his personality changed. He had always been different, but from that moment on he was like a knife. Knife man.

On the way out, Friendly asked me what had happened. I glanced at Belén and said that I would tell him later.

"Sounds good. We'll text," said Friendly.

Belén turned to face me.

"That was great. Your friends are cool. I don't know what happened. I hope they play again." In my head, I replayed the moment we almost kissed, her warm breath settling like dew over my face, her eyes fixed on my mouth, leaning in in slow motion, and then Mario's outburst. She said, "Alright, see you later," and she kissed me on the mouth as if she had known I was incapable of once again creating the right atmosphere. It was a kiss with closed lips, no tongue. Her lips were moist and soft.

Friendly said, "I like you two."

He nodded and they walked away.

At Mario's house, after unloading the instruments, the

three of us sat down to drink Legui. We sat at the table. All that was missing was a game of Risk.

"I don't regret anything," Mario said, as if he had been silently arguing with all his inner Marios. The various knife men covered in blood, screaming and killing each other inside his chest. "I told you, Red. I told you right then."

"I didn't think you were serious, idiot."

"I'm always serious."

"Now we have to get a new bassist," Red said.

"Find a singer too. This isn't for me. I take on the role and it chews me up and spits me onto the floor."

"You're not quitting. This is our band."

"What band? We don't even have a name."

"We have to think of a name," I said, perking up.

"It's hard," Mario said. "It has to be, like, something that people type in to search for porn."

"Something like Pamela Anderson Naked," I said without really thinking, associating it with amateur videos, Baywatch, the Tommy Lee video, and my hidden *Playboys*.

They looked at each other and smiled, but they didn't say anything. I didn't either.

Mario, bottle in hand, shouted, "We're Pamela Anderson Naked and we're going to fuck your brains!"

We laughed and drank.

Then, more quietly, Mario said. "You need to play the bass."

Red strummed his unplugged Strat and showed me the chord progressions of the songs. He said they weren't really punk, and they weren't really grunge. He didn't know what they were exactly, but they came from somewhere deep inside of him.

"I can't play anything," I said, not getting my hopes up. Sometimes Mario said things just to say them.

But if Red had said it, then it was different. He told me he was going to teach me the parts; that I had to play because we were friends. My friends needed a bass player, and that's all there was to it.

"Besides, I didn't like having a bassist that played better than me, and you don't have anything better to do. I'll pick up a bass tomorrow," he said, and we spent a few hours writing down the chord progressions.

Mario fell asleep before I did. It must have been the first time in the history of our friendship. I was meeting a sleeping Mario for the first time. I was dead tired, my head spinning. Red passed out on the couch, holding his guitar. I was hungry. I opened the fridge, and the smell of something rotten burned my nostrils. A tomato with a patch of white mold rotted next to a piece of cooked beef. A White Horse bottle, filled with water. A dozen flans—I checked the expiration date, which had passed three months ago. There was a plate of empanadas. I hesitated, but I grabbed them because the pastry part seemed fine, though everything bad might have just been hidden inside. My phone made the low-battery noise. I looked up Belén's number as quickly as I could, and I memorized it. The phone died. I threw the food and the phone in the trash.

The stench of rot emanated from the trash can, filling the kitchen and the rest of the house. An empty bottle of Legui on the table and a few flies buzzing in circles. The suitcase my parents had lost on their vacation sat on the floor in the corner next to my backpack. It had a ridiculous little lock on it. I could see my father desperately tearing the whole garage apart looking for it. My mother telling him that it was there. Him yelling that he couldn't find it. Her insisting that he not be so helpless. Him searching everything again, calling her a fucking drunk. Yogabriela in the bath, eyes closed and the door locked. Her husband playing piano in the living room with his porcelain fingers and shiny bald head. The country club kids riding their bikes all day long. Lourdes in her maid's room, sitting on the bed, a picture of Saint Cajetan on the bedside table. And me, here, not knowing what came next, mocking my own fear, surrounded by this horrible smell. I opened the door and the place started to air out. I took out the garbage. It was the first time in my life I had ever done it.

I was tired. I threw a thick quilt on the floor. I was going to sleep heavily. The floor wasn't too hard. Maybe it would correct my posture that had gotten so bad from sitting in front of the computer. I tried to sleep, but the suitcase was calling out to me. I tried to open it by hitting the lock against the floor, then by smashing the leg of a chair against it. I tried to slam the bedroom door on it, but the point of impact was imprecise. The door just hit the suitcase. I searched for something a little more forceful, a hammer, an ax, a bazooka, anything. In one of the kitchen drawers I found one of those mallets that people use to flatten milanesas. It seemed just as likely that Mario would have a proton accelerator. The first time I tried, I missed and hit the floor. The second time, nothing. Then I got desperate and gave the lock a series of blows before it finally broke open.

The guys slept through it. I'd have to get rid of the suitcase first thing in the morning. I'd never been so tired. From the floor, I could see how dirty everything was. The sun shone through the broken slats of the blinds. There were spiderwebs under the couch. I repeated Belén's number. My eyes closed. I dove into the void inside me.

Mat Guillan is an Argentine writer and editor. His published works include the novel *Lo que no esperan de mi* (UOiEA! Editorial, 2021), the collection of pop essays *En busca del robot poeta* (self-published, 2019), and the following stories: *Diario de Tayrona* (self-published, 2021) and *Leche fría para almorzar* (self-published, 2021). Additionally, he is a director of UOiEA! Editorial and has translated the work of American writers Sam Pink and Jeremy Robert Johnson. He is the writer of the short film *Superdulce*, which won an award from the Argentine National Institute of Cinema and Audiovisual Arts, and he is a lyricist for the Argentine rock band AURA.

conejomutante.com

OTHER VERY FINE TITLES FROM
TRIDENT PRESS

Let's Walk Together: Stories and Poems in Quechua
by Elva Ambía Rebatta & the Quechua Collective of New York

Tendrel: A Meeting of Minds
by Anne Waldman

Launch Me to the Stars, I'm Finished Here
by Nick Gregorio

Echo Chamber
by Claire Hopple

Dead Mediums
by Dan Leach

Until the Red Swallows It All
by Mason Parker

Tourorist: How I Failed to Find Myself in Southeast Asia
by Tanner Ballengee

The Only Living Girl in Chicago
by Mallory Smart

Selftitled
by Nicole Morning

The Green and the Gold
by Bart Schaneman

Las Vegas Bootlegger
by Noah Cicero

Western Erotica Ho
by Bram Riddlebarger

With a Difference
by Francis Daulerio and Nick Gregorio

America at Play
by Mathias Svalina

The Silence is the Noise
by Bart Schaneman

Sixty Tattoos I Secretly Gave Myself at Work
by Tanner Ballengee

Cactus
by Nathaniel Kennon Perkins

Major Diamonds Nights & Knives
by Katie Foster

it gets cold
by hazel avery

Blood-Soaked Buddha/Hard Earth Pascal
by Noah Cicero

Los Espíritus
by Josh Hyde

The Pocket Austin Osman Spare

The Soul of Man Under Socialism
by Oscar Wilde

*Propaganda of the Deed:
The Pocket Alexander Berkman*

The Pocket Aleister Crowley

The Pocket Peter Kropotkin

The Pocket Emma Goldman

www.tridentcafe.com/trident-press-titles

www.ingramcontent.com/pod-product-compliance
Lightning Source LLC
Chambersburg PA
CBHW021718190726
48289CB00008B/2583